Until The Water Runs Clear

Rich Hayden

Until The Water Runs Clear by Rich Hayden

Until the Water Runs Clear - Copyright 2019 - Rich Hayden

Formatting by Rik – Wild Seas Formatting
http://www.WildSeasFormatting.com

ISBN# 978-0-9963969-5-0

Table of Contents

Chapter One: Savages

1. The Nothing Men

My name is Paul Parker, I am twenty years old, and, twenty years ago, I didn't exist. That all seems to be on the square, doesn't it? The arithmetic, I mean. But there's a variable in there that upsets a seemingly ordinary calculation. That variable is my skin. This skin of mine, and all that is contained within, can testify to the abuse and wear that forty-four years are capable of dealing out. This discrepancy wasn't never lost to me. I always knew there was more back there, things blacked from my recollection by the shadows that hung over my mind. But after a time, I forgot to mourn for the things that I could no longer remember. I grew and changed anew. I paid no never mind to the mystery of the forgotten man I used to be.

I am one man, and that there's the cosmic tragedy of it all. But I have had the rare opportunity to lead two separate lives. Well, that ain't quite right. I caught a break somewhere along the way that afforded me a respite from my initial life. That respite came to be known as Paul Parker. Two damned silly words, devoid of meaning and applied to an individual that even my own eyes regarded as a stranger. But what the hell? The name was as good as any. It fit, for a time. It was two long decades that proved too damn short.

I was born twenty-four years before my friend Paul Parker came along. I harbor no desire to speak of who I really am, although, in time, I will. I never much liked me. Not much of no one really ever had, not that I can blame 'em. Some of those I crossed along the way probably would've liked Paul. But, circumstances being what they are, some folks came around too soon and Paul came 'round too late. Oh, I gotta let Paul go. I guess somewhere inside, I always knew the day would come when I would have to put him in the ground and resume the existence he so graciously interrupted. I feel like I'm attending my own funeral, but there's to be no body. Damn sure won't be no rest.

Before Paul Parker was given a name, he was born much the same as all the rest of us. His arrival was bloody and ushered in with screams of pain. I remember how the light hurt his eyes. I was afraid and he was confused. Now he's gone, forevermore a memory in the minds of others. As for me, I remain. I, too, exist in the minds of others, but for wholly different reasons. And this is where me and Paul must say our goodbyes and part. He has a future. He will go on living in the hearts of those who once loved him. I will go on living, too, for a while, but all I got is the past. And what is it that they say about the past? It always comes back 'round, don't it?

The drink can be given up, but the damage lingers. The whores can be cast aside, but the diseases courted will pay no mind to morally-mended ways. The price can be ignored, but one day the bill's gonna come due. When you throw something away, you make damn sure it's not a boomerang. I'm comin' back, but not as a man. I will return as retribution. I will complete that which is unfinished. I will set right that which is crooked. Woe for the bastards. Ain't nothing can save 'em now.

2. Drowning In A River Of Chains

Before the sudden appearance of Paul Parker, I was known as Kellen Black. That name feels much more appropriate. Not better, mind you, but it sums me up with all its darkness and hard edges.

I was born in the burnt-out garage of an old Texaco service station. Baptized in muddy water and gasoline, I was set up on the curb. Abandoned at day one, I was left to die, hungry and cold under an empty sky. Not even the moon and all them distant stars wanted nothing to do with me.

That's where it all kicked off for me, and that is where it should have ended. But, like most all plagues and pestilence, I lived on to torment all that I would touch. My formative years were spent as a ward of wolves and common thieves. My home, as it were, was an old roadside inn located in rural Ohio. Those in charge ran numbers, trafficked intoxicants, and filed the serial numbers off of guns. It was the type of place that served potato wine in plastic cups. Female affection, of the distant and dead-eyed variety, could be purchased for fifty dollars.

The details of how I came to reside in such a place are unknown to me. I had no steady caregiver, and I was never paid much mind by anyone. To this day, it is a mystery to me as to why my presence there was tolerated. I can only suppose that my residency offered those in charge some advantage I have since forgotten, or was never made privy to in the first place. The specifics don't matter. It all comes down to nothing, anyway.

By the fifteenth year of my life, or, at least, an agreed upon approximation of such, I was on my own. Why I left, or if I was cast out, I can't really say. All I know is that one night I was there in my closet, asleep in my shoes among the smells of stale cigarettes and mold, and the next morning, I was on the road. I started on down the asphalt with only the clothes I wore. No money. No identification. Nothing was my most cherished possession. A birth certificate, a social security number, the receipts of my American existence, they were small luxuries I did not possess. Much the same as Paul Parker would later discover about himself, I did not officially exist.

I came of age out there in the wilderness, my childhood and adolescence extinguished by the constant desperation for base necessities. When it was hot, the cruel sun baked the moisture from my skin and evaporated the pitifully small reservoir of tears held within me. The acidic rain became my shower. Sin and shame were my soap, both of which I liberally applied to myself. My dinners were pulled from garbage cans and stolen from the mouths of those as unfortunate as I. By night I made my bed among mud and weeds. I regressed to a primal, bestial creature, but I also stood as a testament to evolution through natural selection. In the wild, among beasts, it is survival of the fittest. But maybe that all ain't quite so, as I have never been fully fit of mind or body. I saw one choice for myself back then. Predator or prey. I much preferred to be the former, and so I warmed to the challenge offered up by survival of the fiercest.

It was about four years, to the best that I can figure, that I spent on my own. I made my hunting grounds in and around small industrial towns that had been crippled by poverty and forgotten by the charitable winds of progress. I never had no desire to try my luck on them of better means. That all seemed too much of a bother. The law figures into play too often in such places and tends to favor folks that are well-to-do. Sure, those living high up on the gilded hills have nicer shit, but that's all anything ever was to me, shit. The rich man has more shit than the poor man, so I just figured on taking from a larger number of poor men. The rich woman's ass don't feel no different than the poor woman's. I went for the low-hanging fruit. Things gone rotten always held a certain appeal for me.

During my solo run of criminal exploits, I looted any store and home that seemed easy enough to knock over. Every window I spied came to my eyes as an image of opportunity. Rocks are rough, glass is refined. I came to view bricks and stones as having one purpose: to disfigure. I was of the earth. I was ugly. There was something about the perfection of a glass pane that angered and insulted me. I developed something of an addiction to the action of smashing my way into buildings. The weight of something crude in my hand, the burn of my muscles as I performed my act, the sound of glass as it shattered. It was pure euphoria. After a time, I rarely even tested doors to see whether or not they were locked. There was just no fun in that, no destruction.

I can't rightly put a reason on why I stole half the things I did. The use and functionality of my spoils was secondary. It was the acquisition of ill-gotten goods that sustained me. Every week, I must have thrown out the majority of my take. I relished that part, too. I knew my share of skid-row bums and street junkies. They could have benefitted from my discards, but I wasn't no charity. In a way, with my wastefulness, I was taking from them as well. Every item I cast into the river or set on fire I counted as a new theft. I even kept a tally, for a while, of those I had taken from and of those I had summarily deprived of comfort, until the math overran my uneducated mind.

With my ever-increasing need to dispose of my excess bounty, I discovered the infernal joy found in the union of gasoline and matchsticks. Adolescents are impressionable by nature. Maybe this is why I took such a fascination for arson. Or maybe it was something deeper than that. Mankind has always been drawn to the flame. We may tread a bit more carefully than the humble moth, but we, too, find the characteristics of fire mesmerizing. If I could hazard a guess why, I would say our obsession stems from the risks that always come shackled to the time-honored tradition of playing with fire. It's the mixing of curiosity and arrogance that conspire to cause a common sparkler to burn the flesh of a child, and it's this same concoction that wipes scores of men from existence through warfare. We just can't help ourselves.

My personal affair with immolation started small. Trashcan fires and homemade bombs of oily rags and butane bottles kept me entertained for a stretch, but I was just warming up, in a manner of speaking. I soon moved on to cars. At first, I just lit up a few salvage yard vehicles. This provided amusement, but I was never in it for the laughs. What I really needed was to take from others. Now, I suppose, it wasn't so much about the destruction. It was about what the destruction represented. My ability to decide the fate of a stranger's property.

I moved on quickly. Any car left unattended, whether along a dark street or parked comfortably away from a potential witness to my new hobby, was a target. I set fire to abandoned buildings and residences alike, never bothering to consider the people that may have been sheltered inside. On more than one occasion, my efforts burned for hours, leaving nothing but piles of smoldering ash to testify to the rage that bore them.

I have no knowledge of whether or not my blazes seriously injured or killed anyone. That bothers me. Well, that fact eventually served to bother Paul Parker extensively, but it also bothers the man I really am and the boy I used to be. We all have different reasons why. As for the boy I once was, he wasn't finding the high to his satisfaction. No, I needed verification of the pain I was hoping to mete out. Suffering is a sensation that inanimate objects cannot experience. I needed more. I needed blood.

This part got tricky. A truck just sits there as it is vandalized. Once thrown out, possessions do not return looking for vengeance. People are quite a different puzzle. They're a challenge, and that challenge was the dope I craved. People fight back. They resist, scream, and call the authorities. Or, worse, they call their friends and attempt to administer justice as they see fit. Those were just some sticky details I was willing to face in my pursuit of nocent satisfaction. Compassion, I could not find it in me. I was a predator that aspired to be a conqueror. Eventually, my aspirations would set me into the role of executioner.

I was a healthy young man back then, strong and tall, albeit somewhat malnourished. But even the growls of my stomach and the aches of my muscles were turned into an advantage. I was always sore for one reason or another. Plainly put, I never felt good. I sharpened my ferocity against the hard truth of my discomforts. I was not made perfect, however, as I lacked experience.

Unseasoned in the ways and wiles of personal combat, I took my share of beatings. I've had teeth knocked out, my nose has been broken, and my eyes were probably black for months on end. I never got stitches, but that don't mean nothing much. I've been cut, stabbed, and slashed. All them wounds I went about mending with superglue, rags, and tape. I've suffered infections due to the punishments I had been dealt. I've had my wrists sprained and the ankles twisted. It should go without mention that I can attest to the agony of broken bones. My early career as a thug didn't afford me the opportunity to place many notches in the win column. But there was one thing that always happened after I took a thrashing: I got up.

There was some part of me that relished injury. I grew accustomed to pain. I grew tolerant of it. I started to look less like a boy and more like the man I wanted to be. A scarred and dangerous man. I looked like a tree that had been planted on a slope and fertilized in sludge and chemical run-off. I came up crooked and rough. Ugly and unwashed, I was finally developing into the intimidation machine I aspired to be. I took pride in bruises and loved the look of dried blood under my fingernails. My hair grew out wiry and an unkempt beard seemed to appear on my face overnight. Almost like it had been beaten out of me. I wore it like an advertisement of the death of the child I no longer was.

Now, as much as I had been familiarized with what it feels like to lose a fight, the sensation of winning felt a great deal better. I would pick fights with strangers for no reason at all, and I attacked bums as they slept on the streets under blankets of cardboard. I had no sense of virtue and felt no inclination to inject fairness into my battles. If my opponent had just his fists, it was all the better that I had a pipe. I employed knives and discovered that rocks could be used for more than just breaking windows. But, without any reservation, I can say that my favorite kind of weapon was anything heavy and blunt. Clubs, metal poles, sticks, even, if they were of the right constitution. I never did use guns, though. Something about them just wasn't personal enough for me. I needed to feel the beatings I administered. I liked working for it, seeing the disfigurement that my labor brought.

I know I put a good number of people in the hospital. Well, I can't say for certain if that's where they went, but the damage

I inflicted was usually sufficient to warrant a trip to the emergency room. There was this one hobo, I never knew his handle, but I think about him from time to time. He was a big bastard, a good six inches taller than me, and he probably weighed over three hundred pounds. Over some trivial insult I can no longer remember, we went rounds in an alleyway. It was night and a cold rain was falling from the sky. I was up against a titan, and as I lay on the ground with my face in dirty water and blood in my eyes, I thought about scampering away. I was overmatched, that was clear, but I had stamina and youth on my side.

Once my adversary had tired of pummeling me, he went back to his corner of stink and piss to resume drinking his wine. I crawled upright and pulled my knees to my chest. I shuddered and experienced spears of pain with every labored breath. Seemingly without warning, an ejection of vomit shot from my mouth. Colors that weren't there clouded my vision. In the quiet aftermath of my punishment, I heard as he chuckled at my distress. With curses on his tongue, he shouted some nonsense at me as I staggered away and out of sight. I was angry, sure, and my pride was wounded as deep as my body. I felt something else, too. I felt invigorated. I had tripped my way into a dragon's lair, and I was fixed on slaying the beast.

I walked under burnt-out lampposts and over buckled concrete without direction. I poked my nose into a few Dumpsters along the way until I found the Excalibur required for the task fate had offered to me. I pulled an iron pipe into the light of the moon and examined my instrument. It was rusty and uncomfortable to hold, and one end was broken into a crude point. I was shivering, but my palms began to sweat as excitement coursed through my veins and gave to me a new sense of warmth. Taking a few practice swings, I carried on and made my way back to the entrance of the alley.

Through the vapor that rose from the sewer lids, I emerged like a warrior of old passing beyond the mists of a haunted forest. Half asleep and drunk, that vagrant behemoth never knew what hit him. I brought my wrath down upon him in a flurry of blows, all of which found their intended mark. He slumped over without a sound, and I laid down a few more strikes, until the rough pipe began to bite at the flesh of my palms. With rust on my hands and adrenaline flooding my heart, I flung the pipe into the air and shouted to the empty sky above. I howled like a madman, a lunatic transformed into a creature, as the pipe rang off the ground.

To this day, I walk without the knowledge of whether or not I had killed the goliath. I cannot claim to have verification of if I can rightly be classified as a murderer. But he weren't the only one, far from it. I engaged in so much wanton violence in those days that, odds are, I have killed someone. That's where the safe money rests, anyway, on me carrying the deaths of others around my neck. The thing is, the final outcomes of my victories didn't hold much interest for me. If I never saw a man again, he was as good as dead to me. But I got no more patience for the mystery. The nagging uncertainty of my murderous merit. To assuage my guilt, I guess I can entertain the fantasy that my hands are clean. But that way of thinking just feels like a knotted up ball of lies, as fantasy is a luxury I do not possess. It's time to face the truth of what I am and what I will yet be.

Up to that point, and for many years after, my life was like a river of chains. Heavy events, linked together, all coated in rust and decay. Bitter misfortunes tumbled over one another, always tugging, dragging forth the next line of sorrows. I was being crushed under the weight of my own existence, a force too massive for me to overcome, never allowing me to gulp down any breath of relief. Sinking under the iron weave of reality, I came into adulthood. It was right about this time that I met Polly.

3. Toxicity

I never had much use for women. Even as a boy morphing into a man, I found little desire for sex. The hollow within me where lust should have been housed seemed a curious riddle. But the more I peeled back the layers of this mystery, the less puzzling it became. I believed, rather erroneously, that what drove my actions was a thirst for the primal. That wasn't never quite it, though. Sexual intercourse is primal, but it can also be pleasurable. The sensation of pleasure, the emotions that come grafted to it, always unbalanced me. What I sought most was pain. Any expression of it, any affliction, would do. Whether portioned out to strangers who crossed into my path, or done to me by others, the feeling of pain was the only stimulus that drove me. To my damaged mind, rape seemed the next logical step to take.

Rape, I'm told, is often about the quest for power, to feel absolute dominion over the vulnerable. This wasn't the case for me. For all that I was, and all that I fancied myself, being powerful didn't linger among my other delusions. What appeal does power hold, anyway? It's nothing more than a blindfold and a bandage. It's a paper wall put up before the knives of time and circumstance that, sooner or later, come to cripple us all.

Like power, sexual desire and satisfaction are fleeting. Sex and power, they're the empty applause breaks built into the play of life. So, without any genuine affection for power or true sexuality, it all came back to pain. Harm or be harmed, those were my choices, and rape afforded me both. Watching a person crumble under my assault, feeling their body go limp once they gave in to the dirty hand fate had dealt them, gave me the most gratification. In those moments, I knew I had carved an injury so deep that it would never fully heal. And then, it was my turn to sink down into suffering.

After I had raped someone, I felt horrible. Not guilty or remorseful, just bad. Sick. I felt tired. I was often shaky and left without clarity of mind. I gained nothing from the act, and that was the purpose: to be emptied out of all but the most persistent of feelings, pain. I raped a couple of men, too. They were both vagrants, one fat, the other pitifully thin, and each stunk of shit and sweat. Once these attacks concluded, much as with the women, I felt awful. With the men, however, there seemed to be an extra layer of filth and shame that stuck to me. I had shattered multiple taboos within the same minutes, and the agony this gave to me almost bestowed upon me a sense of peace. Almost. It was as though I had found a way to spit in the face of god.

Polly came before my vision as common gutter trash. She wore combat boots and a pair of tight jeans cut into shorts. A faded tank top exposed her stomach, as well as the ragged tattoos that had been carved over her biceps. Her hair, blonde and cropped short, was gelled into a field of golden spikes that twinkled in the light of a hot summer morning. She still retained the facial features of a girl, but was wrapped in the rough, sunbaked skin of a mill-town prostitute.

I studied her, my prey, as she paced along the outer limits of a deserted alleyway. She appeared to be alone, but not without purpose. I couldn't make out just what she was doing. I courted the notion that she was looking for a trick to turn. There was something about that thinking that didn't add up. I settled on the assumption that her pacing was symptomatic of an itch. There ain't no alarm clock that can rival the insistency with which the need for narcotics tugs at the mind. There she was, just a junkie girl, hung on a hook. The bait was set and I moved in like a sea creature as it rises from the deep to swallow up the weak things that exist just below the muddied surface.

Her back was turned to me during my advance, and she seemed oblivious to the predator at her heels. But, like the scorpion mouse as it turns to conquer its arachnid adversary, she was upon me before I could strike. Polly stuck me in the gut with a penny knife, and, before I could finish folding to the ground below, her accomplices descended.

Two men emerged from the shadows. One rifled through my pockets while the other took to kicking my ribs in with his boots. My senses were dulled but I could see Polly hovering above me. Her lips was bent into a grin, and her teeth came out to play with every giggle of mad laughter. She really seemed excited by my tribulation. She bounced up and down as a bratty school girl might do when gifted with a pony.

"Fuck 'em up! Fuck 'em up!" I heard that command over and over. Her voice was a record that looped one harsh refrain, keeping time with the blows of my battering.

Left alone, I bled and I cried, feeling that my time to shuffle off to death was at hand. I curled into a ball like the broken animal I was and fell into unconsciousness, a victim, tossed down to the grounds occupied by those I routinely victimized.

I awoke at night. I can't testify that it was the same night. Wounds such as mine don't allow the mind to parse such particulars of the calendar. More immediate, more pressing details of my circumstance bore down over me. The air held a chill and the clouds pissed out rain in sharp bursts. The moisture soaked through my clothes. It raised bumps across my flesh and sent shivers into my bones. As the water pooled, and then ran over my skin, it washed dirt into the puncture Polly had given me. If the initial assault didn't end up killing me, the infection to come surely would. I felt put in my place, like a fat, vicious rat swiftly reminded of a rodent's place in the food chain. God was spitting back.

Stabbed and spit upon, I lived. I won't say that I was healed proper. Healing was something I was never quick to come by, but I lived. Eventually, I got up and kept on. I left my spot on the ground with sickness and ache. I departed with hunger and tremors. I set off down the streets with questions, and, once I sat back down, I was left with nothing but a morbid curiosity about the beast I would later come to know as Polly.

For the better part of two weeks, I wandered the streets in search of Polly. True, I didn't have much else to do, what with my chronic lack of employment and my injuries slowing me down, but finding her was my priority. I knew street life well, as well as most men know their backyards or living rooms. My house was large, but I familiarized myself with every dark corner, crack, and sewer path. After a time, I was even able to recognize the stray dogs as individuals, but Polly proved an elusive creature.

The pain that accompanied my convalescence was slow to dissipate, and its lingering spears made me wholly aware of mortality for the first time. It sounds funny, but I suppose that a sense of invincibility is the last of youth's well-armored follies. I began to reexamine my existence, my way of gettin' things done. I had made a few easy scores for basic human necessities, food, bandages, and such, but I was in a bad way. I couldn't continue on as I was. Even a top predator, once gone lame, becomes a target. I could go on alone no more. I had no want for change, but if I was gonna keep on as a wolf, I needed to join up with a pack.

On past the shuttered factory and burned-out tenement houses, I was out walking the train tracks. I followed the curve of that industrial spine to the edge of town, where disused appliances and broken-down cars get scattered and left to decay. Buzzards circled overhead and wind blew uprooted weeds along the gravel of my path. A small tunnel became visible in the distance. It was a rocky wound that segregated the collapse of failed enterprise from the wilderness beyond. I'm not sure why I kept on toward the tunnel. To the best that I can figure, it must have looked like as good a place as any to eat my lunch. The noontime sun had me sweating bullets, and the scraps I had pulled from the McDonald's Dumpster weren't gonna get no fresher.

I staggered into the shadows of the tunnel and slunk to the damp ground below. From my pocket, I unfolded the wet paper bag that contained what was surely the only food I would consume that day. I pinched the end of the bag and squeezed down the rotten contents into my mouth. Spying a half full bottle of sports drink that sat upright in the shadows, I set about washing down my meal. Slightly ill, but accustomed to such things, I leaned back against the cool stones and exhaled a sign of pain.

"Fuck off!" a voice barked at me from the deeper shadows of the tunnel.

I peered through the darkness to the far end of the tunnel. My eye caught the gleam of a revolver as it had been aimed in my direction. I made not a motion, electing instead to study the source of the threat. It was Polly, no doubt, her blonde spikes sparkling like broken glass in the dirty bands of daylight that bled into the space she occupied. It took me by surprise that she hadn't bothered to look up. I guess she felt confident in the one-eyed stare of her gun being sufficient to chase away the unwanted. She sat with one foot under her, her other leg out straight, as she fumbled with something on the ground. I watched as she leaned forward and gripped a thin band between her teeth. She yanked her head back and pulled the material tight around her arm.

"Hey," she shouted, "I can do this and shoot you at the same time. You got five seconds, dude."

"I been lookin' for you," I said, still on the ground.

"Then that's your mistake. Four," she said.

"I don't mean you no harm."

"Three."

"Look, girl, I'm kinda fucked up right now. I ain't moving, so you go on and shoot me. Or put that thing down and have an easier time of getting your fix."

For the first time, Polly lifted her eyes to me and gave me a quick once-over. Looking into her eyes was like staring into the open mouth of a viper. I knew she meant business, but I also recognized the shift in her face once she settled on me not being worth a pull of her index finger.

"You're lucky I'm almost out, or I'd have popped you already," she said, lowering the gun.

"Don't you think that puts you at a disadvantage? Tellin' me you're low on rounds?" I replied, as I felt the need to test her personality.

"Don't matter, I never miss," she said confidently, pressing a needle into her arm.

"Feel better?" I asked after a moment to allow the junk to set to work on her neural circuitry.

"Oh, fuck, yes," she whispered as she leaned back to match my relaxed pose.

"What's your game?" I asked.

"You ain't too bright, are you, dude? You don't go looking for a suck *after* a junkie's had their fix."

"That's not what I mean. In way of speaking, I'm looking for friends."

This revelation caused Polly to laugh uncontrollably for a spell. I had heard a lot of malicious laughter in my short life, but the noises she made were brand new to me. There weren't a shiver of happiness in the sounds that rippled out from her throat. Her giggling held all the sugar you'd expect to hear from a young girl on the border of adulthood, but there was morbidity and a great weight of disease shackled to her outburst. Her laughter gave me visions of witches as they eat the raw flesh of children.

"This sure as shit ain't no Facebook," she said once she had moderately composed herself.

"Hey, the bottom line is this: I like to steal things. I like to hurt people, and I know you do, too," I said, and lifted my shirt to show Polly the results of her handiwork.

I watched as her eyes got big as her muddled mind tried to sort out if I was real or just a vivid dope dream. She felt around the ground and failed to locate the gun that rested mere inches from her leg. Polly mumbled incoherently. Her eyes rolled back and their lids slid down like elevators designed to escort the damned to hell.

"Nobody wants to be my friend," she said in a slur. Her remark was quiet, and it wasn't meant for me to hear, I knew that much. What she had said was a trickle from the river of pain she harbored inside. I recognized it straight away, the fragility she allowed no one to see. It was the toxicity of junk that had cracked her armor. I started to assemble this puzzle of a girl. She stole away to be alone when it came time for a fix, in an attempt to shield her vulnerability from the eyes of others. After a time, these descents into weakness would force her to put the needle down. But that day was still a long time off.

"Maybe friend ain't the right word to use. I'm just looking for some people to run with. I ain't makin' it out here on my own. Hey, I can't go right. There's no life for me in that," I said, and it sounded to me like a plea.

"Alright. Yeah, fuck it. Whatever, dude." Then, after a pause, she asked, "What's in it for me?"

I didn't answer. I wasn't no charity. Besides, I actually had nothing to offer and felt not the least bit bad about it. I stayed quiet, long enough for Polly to slump over and pass out. As she slept, I thought about the wound she gifted to me. I entertained killing her. It would have been easy, justified, perhaps, and I would finally be able to add a certified killing to my criminal resume. I thought to rape her, but only briefly. She never would have known, and that kinda soured the temptation. The pursuit of causing agony was what drove me anyhow, and I doubt I would have been able to deal additional suffering to her just then. Foolishly, I felt a tiny prick of sympathy for Polly. I let her sleep. I made a mistake.

We walked back to town, towards the ash-black smokestacks and crumbling facades of abandoned high-rises. Over the buckled asphalt and through the stink of mid-summer, we got to talking. Polly was a high school dropout. A run-away that come from Cleveland with nothing more than I had when I was expelled from my roadside orphanage. Her story was familiar and mildly interesting, but I didn't ask too many questions. It wasn't out of some sense of respect that I kept to myself. I was confident that I could fill in the blanks without interrogation. Mommy had no time for her, no doubt. There was probably an uncle, maybe even an older brother, that got handsy with her at a tender age. Addiction was surely woven into her DNA and Polly certainly struggled under the strain of undiagnosed mental disorders. Had I asked, it would have been the same sob story. I couldn't really have cared less. What did spark my curiosity though, was how she kept those blonde spikes gelled sharp and tight under the summer sun.

"You got any smokes, man?" she asked, while checking her pockets for a pack.

"I got a few cigarillos I found while knocking over a car about a week back. They kinda suck."

"I've had worse in my mouth. Come on," she said, motioning for me to hand one over.

"Take the pack."

"You ain't kidding. These taste like shit," said Polly after she took a drag. "So, you're not pissed about me knifing you? I'd be on fucking fire."

"I was, for a while. But then I realized that you were just like me. Normal people are boring. You at least seemed exciting to me," I said.

"I'll take you to my place. You can meet Wayne and Bill, that was them dudes that busted you up. But this," she said, while rapidly directing her finger back and forth in the empty air between us, "this ain't gonna be no Bonnie and Clyde thing, if that's what you're thinking."

"No…" I started to answer, but Polly interrupted me as it seemed the drug haze was beginning to lift from her.

"I'm mostly into chicks, anyway," she began. "I mean, I'll turn a trick to score sometimes. I don't consider myself a hooker. It's more like a favor for a favor thing. If there's nothing to do, I'll take a dick. So, I don't know, I guess I'm not that picky, but I ain't nobody's girlfriend. I hate the way that sounds. It sounds so fucking gay."

"No, that ain't my scene. I can't imagine attaching myself to someone else like that," I said.

"Right? Like how fucking awful is that? Hey, let's go to Cheesecake Factory and then binge watch Big Bang," she said, mockingly, and made some gestures that I imagine were meant to look dorky.

"That's too bad. I was hoping you were the kinda chick that I could take to Pottery Barn." I said this flatly, but Polly giggled. My comment triggered an exchange between us where we discussed all the inane things we were going to do as part of our make-believe relationship. We both got to laughing. I think we were both hurt and confused by the sensation.

Once we crossed into the town limits, we walked through the mire and into the muck. I had kept residence and slept in some truly awful places, but Polly's home was where sorrow yielded to misery, waste was churned into sludge, and common dirt was swapped out in favor of true filth.

She, along with Wayne and Bill, squatted in an apartment located over an abandoned laundromat down a dead-end street. The entire block was deserted. Polly explained that a flash flood had come through a few years before and stripped the buildings of all functionality. All that was needed was for a great big mudslide to come and bury the whole goddamned thing.

She led me up a rickety fire escape. The handrails were bent and the steps were treacherous. Rot and rust made the metal thin in spots, while in others, strips of steel hung out sharp and jagged. We came to a door built from warped plywood. Polly kicked the door free from the jamb and welcomed me inside.

The light was low, the only illumination from the streaks of sunlight that found their way in through the windows and the cracks in the ceiling. A heavy collection of dust particles floated in the amber rays and the small room stunk of cigarettes and chemicals.

There weren't no working utilities, but Bill had boosted a portable electric generator that served to power a small TV, a few lamps, a hot plate, and an old Xbox. The generator sat just outside the makeshift door, while the fumes from the exhaust took to collecting inside. There was two tank-top propane heaters stashed in the corner for when winter come. A store of water jugs sat in a bathtub full of rust rings and mildew. Polly told me the water was bad. They only used it to flush the toilet. If I was fixing to wash up, she told me they kept a plastic kiddie pool on the roof. The water warmed in the sun, and there was a bottle of dish soap and a large car sponge up there as well.

I left her to the dark chambers of the apartment below and

emerged back into the sunlight. The roof was flat and hotter than the diseased breath of devils. The surface coating was dry and cracked but fresh tar had been sloshed over the worst parts in a failed effort at keeping the rain away. I skimmed my fingers through the still water of the little pool. It was half empty and hosted a layer of fallen leaves and drowned bugs. I squirted soap into the sponge and set to lathering up as best I could. The water felt near boiling, but it felt good to scrub my face and run some liquid through my hair. I scrubbed away at the remainder of my stab wound and glanced around my surroundings.

At street level, the town always looked sick to me, but what I saw from on high was different. From this vantage, our village appeared to be a corpse. Long since dead, there was nothing left but decay and a skeleton of rusted steel beams. The many disused houses seemed to be a thousand eye sockets, each one hollowed out. I focused on the river in the distance and my eyes followed it as it curved away and into the hills. It had a brownish-blue tint, and the sight made me think of it as a bloated vein. Engorged with toxins, the river looked primed to burst and wash additional filth down onto us. I snorted back an excess of mucus that had collected in my nose, took a piss, and made my way back down into the apartment.

Polly introduced me to Wayne and Bill, who were sitting next to each other on an old couch, playing some racing game on the Xbox. Neither one acknowledged me. I took a seat on an upturned milk crate and studied the group. All of them, even Polly, were nearly naked. This was understandable, as the heat of the day turned their place into an oven, but something about this sat funny with me. It was the way that both of them guys never so much as glanced over at Polly. It was like they knew better. I figured, straight off, that each had fucked Polly, at one time or another, but any sex was surely on her terms only. It was the damnedest thing. They both seemed clearly uncomfortable, afraid, even, of her presence. I rubbed the damage at my side and felt lucky.

"Hey, faggots," said Polly to her roommates, snapping her

fingers to get their attention. "Did you hear me? This is Kellen. Either one of you dicks wanna say hi?"

Like dogs trained to obey the whistle and fear the beating, both Wayne and Bill offered whispered greetings in my general direction. Bill gave a nod of his head and an uneasy smile that spoke to me with all the subtly of a highway signboard. It was a warning. He was telling me that all was due to go bad, and, with Polly in the mix, bad always came sooner than later. I recognized his gesture of kindness right off, as kindness was as rare to me as sunlight at the underbelly of the sea. But fuck him. I didn't need no charity, and I didn't need no protection courtesy of the 110 pounds of nervous uncertainty that was poor Bill. I just smiled back and wrapped myself in the horror he displayed as I went about staring at Polly's tits.

Not much else came to pass that evening. I didn't mind. My usual hunger for criminal mischief hadn't yet returned. I suppose it spilled right out when Polly's little knife forced me to acknowledge my mortality. Assuming the habits of the languorous was a welcome turn of character for me. True leisure was what I needed most that day, even if such a break was inside a summer-baked apartment that stunk of mold. I gave in to my lethargy and slept. As I nodded off, I felt like a boar in a butcher shop.

I awoke sometime the next afternoon, mildly surprised that Polly had resisted the urge to slaughter me in my sleep. She was the type to do such a thing out of boredom. She was the type, my type. I found myself alone and went about helping myself to whatever they had left behind. I gnawed my way through a bag of potato chips that had grown a bit soft. I washed my breakfast back with warm lemonade. The carton had been kicked under a table. It wore a cloak of dust and spider webs, but it was unopened. Sometimes, it's the little miracles.

As dusk approached, I began rummaging through the cardboard boxes that held the possessions of my new roommates. Not much interested me. It was mostly the same old junk, a few CDs, ragged and obnoxious clothing, and assorted trinkets of little value. There were some pictures, old photographs, and yellowed letters that I couldn't be bothered to read. And then, I found an ID card of Polly's. Initially, this discovery was bereft of meaning. I studied it all the same. Curiosity, and nothing deeper, kept my eyes keen to her identification. The picture couldn't have been more than a couple of years old, but it was certainly taken before Polly got taken by the needle. That cold, hateful stare filled her eyes, but her skin was clean, her cheeks still full with the fat left over from childhood. It was then that I read her full name: Polly Parker. That all meant less to me than the grime that collected within the treads of my shoes. However, many years later, when I assumed the name Paul Parker, I would come to realize that Polly had a much deeper impact on me than I'd care to admit. I still can't rightly point to a reason why.

The dark of the night came and brought with it excess humidity and the harsh calls of insect chatter. I was still alone, and I began to wonder if my prospective accomplices had already abandoned me. I stepped out onto the rusted fire escape and breathed in the raw air of summer. The action of sucking back a deep breath caused me to wince, but pain was such a familiar sensation that I felt a small measure of happiness from its needling. I watched as the moon cast its glow over the broken expanse of the town I called home. The light washed over the mess like a policemen's flashlight as he inspects the wreckage of a crime scene. Ugliness was everywhere.

I suppose I was feeling physically better. Not well, of course, but better. Well enough for the desire to disfigure and vandalize to seep back into me. It was in that moment that I sighted the outline of two figures as they staggered down the street and toward my position. I recognized one of them as Bill right off. His walk was jerky. It seemed he couldn't do a damned thing without twitchin'. The other beside him had to be Wayne. Who else could it be?

I then got to thinking about the relationship between the

pair and I couldn't make no real sense of it. Bill, he was like a mouse with a bum leg that went about tripping into the domain of snakes. His survival rested solely on his abject willingness to obey his betters without question. That was enough for him to earn Polly's protection, but I never saw what Wayne stood to gain from allowing Bill to slow things down. What was more, Bill was the kind who had the tendency to fuck things up. He was just that way. He was meek, but he was also a complicator with all his frailty and indecision. I knew these tiresome traits would dawn on Polly sooner or later, if they hadn't already. That was why I guessed that Bill hadn't been runnin' with Polly for very long. Wayne, however, he must have come from further back.

Wayne, it seemed, was just that sorry sort who needs a friend. Most anyone would do, but I had my suspicions about most people's willingness to stick with Wayne. He seemed the type who always got left behind, left out, abandoned, and, certainly worst of all, ignored. He needed a shadow, a lesser version of himself that would stay around no matter what. His weakness disgusted me, but, as the night wore on, my judgment softened as I saw something more rise to the surface.

It sure did pain me to admit this, but Wayne was *fun*. He was a big, goofy bastard that smelled of body odor. His laugh was an obnoxious bellow and his words were often strangled by some unfortunate speech impediment. He wasn't fat enough to be intimidating and he was too unfortunate looking to catch the eye of most any woman. But, hell, he was a good dude. It began to puzzle me. Was this really the same guy who had tried to cave my ribcage in just a few ticks back? And that's when the realization hit me: this wasn't the same guy. A variable had changed. Polly wasn't around. With her off doing whatever malfeasance psychopathic junkie girls get up to, the authentic Wayne was permitted to surface.

He was outgoing and inquisitive, although he was too much of a spaz to wait on proper answers to his queries. I didn't care. I had no interest in sharing my feelings. Bill didn't care either. So long as conversation randomly involved him, he was content. And what was better? Wayne didn't actually have an interest in conducting a proper discussion. No reciprocation required. If others were willing to sit around and tolerate the nonsense that tumbled from his mouth, he was as happy as Death in a death camp.

"Kellen!" Wayne shouted my name, as he was wont to do. The sound seemed to amuse him. He shouted my name again, a bit more gleefully, as he directed his whole arm straight out from his body. He pointed a finger to me and lightly knocked his other hand into the side of his leg, trying, I imagined, to work the rest of the sentence out from his uncooperative mind.

"Kellen!" he announced for a third time, with triumph draped over the last syllable.

"Go on, Wayne. I'm listening."

"I need… I need, I need, I need," he said quickly. "I need to be serious with you for a minute."

I nodded my agreement, but studied Wayne all the same during the silence that followed his declaration. I could see as he was fighting to steady his body, to calm his breath, to straighten his words. He damn sure had something serious he wanted to tell me.

"You need to leave, Kellen," he stated with all the authority of a fifth grader.

"C'mon now, I just got here, man," I said, easily, as I reclined in my seat.

"It's about Polly. You need to leave."

"What about Polly?" I asked.

Wayne didn't answer right away. Bill looked at him and I looked at Bill. He was the vision of an over-cooked string bean, all limp and pathetic. But I noticed something else, too. He wasn't shaking. Somehow, someway, Bill had found it in himself to steady his nerves, or, maybe, he was just that scared.

"Polly, well, she's—" Wayne began, but was cut off by Bill's whimpering.

"Shh, Wayne, don't," he pleaded.

"Hey, Bill, shut the fuck up. The adults are talking," I said.

"So…sorry, Kellen." And that was Bill. I insulted him and he apologized.

"Well, like I was saying, or gonna say. I was starting to say, you know? About Polly?"

"Yeah, Wayne, I remember. What? What about Polly?" I asked.

"She killed this girl, Kellen," said Wayne swiftly. He turned his head away, as though looking off into the distance could shield him from further conversation.

"And?" I asked. "I think I've killed people. You guys tried to kill me. I already put it together that Polly ain't no angel. What's the big deal?"

"Sorry, Kellen. We just needed money," said Bill in a whisper.

"Well, you didn't kill me. You're forgiven, alright?"

"Alright," he said, and smiled, seemingly content with the absolution I offered to him.

"This was a girl, man. Like, a little girl," Wayne said. "She didn't even have nothing. We…we didn't want nothing to do with it. Polly, Pol, she just kinda started fucking this kid up. There was no reason. None! No reasons, Kellen."

"Yeah, okay, I got it. So, what'd Polly do? C'mon, man, I need details, here. If you're warning me about Polly, I need the specifics, right?" I wanted to dig, but I honestly didn't care about how it all went down. I was just delighting in making Bill uncomfortable.

"Polly took her gun," said Wayne as he grabbed one of the Xbox controllers to use as a prop. "And she whipped the girl. Not like a whip, but like with a gun, you know? Gun whip. Gun whipping. Bill, is that right?"

"Pistol whipped?" I offered, dryly.

"Pistol whipped!" echoed Wayne. He rose from his seat and slashed the air with the controller. Momentarily, he was bubbly and joyous, but soon crashed back down from the gravity of his tale. "It was real sad. It…it was mean."

"Huh?" I said to myself, and then, to the others, "well, I guess it's a good thing I'm no little girl."

Wayne remained silent and still, but Bill burst into a fit of nervous laughter. I smiled at him and the wider I smiled, the more obnoxious he became. Just to toy around with him, I suddenly dropped my expression to one of stony disapproval. I relished the way he instantly shut up. He looked scared again, and lost, like a kitten subjected to the cacophony created from the whir of a vacuum cleaner. It was in that moment that I come to realize why Polly kept him around. He was just too much fun to fuck with.

So, Polly went and killed a little girl. That was something I actually had to process. I didn't stress my mind trying to come up with reasons why, or justifications and the like. Wayne already told me that reason played no part in the affair, and I was inclined to trust his assessment. But there was two things that had a say in Polly's rage: a root cause and an end goal.

I got to thinking about it in this way: a snow-covered road can cause a car to spin out. The driver will then use logic to take the appropriate action of achieving the end goal, which is to not wind up a splattered mess of humanity among the snowflakes. Funny thing is, though, every event has a cause and an end. Reason is never a requirement. It's just a goddamned luxury that some of us can't afford.

It was during this flowery bit of thinking that I started to unravel the terrible mystery that was Polly. I suppose I already knew why she put the pain to the girl. It was just her nature. Polly was a semi-pretty package, but she was nothing more than a mold of a girl that had been poured up with pain. But in sighting the desires that her wrath sought to accomplish, I began to peel back her monstrous layers. I concluded that the unfortunate little girl represented to Polly all that she never got to be. Her victim was the embodiment of all the youthful innocence that Polly never got to experience. By all that breathes and crawls, live and dies, Polly could not abide such an insult. When it all went down, she wasn't killing no little girl, she was killing herself. And that revelation gave to me the fact that Polly was, in addition to being a beast, a coward. She was too damn scared to eat her own gun, so she had to go about harming those that looked too much like all she was made to go without.

I was having fun taking Polly apart. Was I on the money? Maybe not exactly, but I was putting enough pieces together to lay cash down on a sure bet. But then something unexpected took place. My thinking curved back to turn its teeth on me. I was made to address a few things. The first, and, amazingly, the easiest to swallow, was that I was a lot like Polly. The things we done, the messes we made, all emanated from the same sewer. I was a broken boy trying to fill every void in me with acts of cruelty. I guess I figured that if I filled enough of them holes, true feeling would have nowhere left to hide and, one day, it would up and leave me altogether.

The second conclusion I was made to draw about myself, the harder one to get down, was that I had a line. This meant that, somewhere, I had a conscience. Sure, my line might have been placed a chain and a fathom further down the road of decency than most folks, but it was there all the same. I thought about murdering a child, without reason and with it, as if there could be reason solid enough to do such a thing. I tried to fantasize on it, but it could not be done. My mind would just scatter away. Children were off limits. To harm one was the ultimate taboo, maybe the only true taboo, as no cause used in the orchestration of their suffering could be justified. Me and my new mates, the whole lot of us, probably deserved to be on the losing end. We deserved to die. But that wasn't always the way. That I can say with confidence having never even known Bill, Wayne, or Polly as children. Because the fact that we were all once children was all the proof I needed. Once upon a time, we deserved to live.

Ah, but the times, they change. Food rots, steel rusts, flesh decays, and people regress back to animals, to beasts, to creatures, to ghouls. All of us had strayed far from anything that warranted compassion or salvation. We were owed it not from others, not even from each other. Not from no one. I knew that's where we were and the others knew it as well. Maybe not explicitly, but it was understood. We were not to be trusted. Oh, how we would all come to face the truth and consequences of our condition in due course.

With all my musings on the subject of reason, logic would suggest that the four reprobates featured in my tale would see about setting the world on fire. In time, I suppose we tried our best, but, mostly, we just sat around.

Malaise was our collective affliction, but that wasn't what kept the four of us relatively quiet. We were new to each other, and, no matter the circumstances, that fact distracted us from serious criminal activity. Like the ordinary kids we never were, we sat around each other, hung out, and generally just fucked around.

Polly became a slave to the quest for dope. She would disappear for days at a time, and, when she did return, sleeping was her most indulged pastime. This wasn't proper rest, of course. She passed out over and into anything the human body can crumple into. It got annoying. She got in the way. One of us was always tripping over her or stepping into a puddle of her puke. She got thin and her color drained out into the gutter. Her hair was a mess and she stunk. When it was warm in the house, she didn't bother with clothes. Now, a naked and intoxicated girl keeping company with three straight males would seem destined to play the part of meat thrown to lions. But that meat was so sour and toxic that me and the other fellows rarely even stole a glance at Polly. She was a junk dumpster.

The plight of Polly seemed to suit Bill just fine, as he allowed his fear of her to melt away with every passing day of her descent. Wayne, that nutty bastard, I don't think he even noticed. He might have been the gregarious type, but he largely existed inside his own head. That must have been a truly terrifying place. But what did I care? Wayne was like a gun, scary to look at, but without a finger to pull the trigger, he was just a big lump. Bill, even if he were the aggressive type, he would be an easy win for a scrapper like me. He knew as much, and he always liked to follow anyway. It weren't so bad, him falling in with people like us. Things could have been worse for Bill. I have no doubt that had that boy been raised in a slaughter house, he would've followed the sheep down to the abattoir.

As for me, I speculate that I just went a little soft. I got lazy. There was more of a roof over my head than I was accustomed to having and I had ready access to the most basic of my needs. I took a corner of the place for myself, where I slept and hid food from the others. We had electricity, most of the time, and, best of all, we were anonymous.

Our street might as well have been cut out of the earth and sewn into the surface of a distant planet. The creatures that we were are just not worth bothering over. We were out of sight and in no one's mind. We became forgotten. If only we would have stayed that way.

When people are young, time seems to fly on by, but the individual days seem to last forever. That don't seem to carry on too well with common sense, but anyone that has spent their youth kicking around with their peers should be able to relate. It's like this: time, once seemingly eternal, up and runs out without warning.

Aside from spending my time on the couch fooling about on the Xbox with Bill and Wayne, I took to drink. My introduction and eventual decline didn't happen the way it typically does for most others. I didn't begin my relationship with the bottle by courting a good buzz with cheap beer. I didn't move on to more sophisticated libations, and I sure never discovered a favored brand. No, I threw down rat piss and kept at it. These days of inebriation cooled my irritability and made my couch-mates easier to tolerate. I still had the urge to dismantle property and inflict suffering on the unsuspecting, but the booze robbed me of action. It was easier to just stay home and get drunk. There was, however, an unforeseen development during my dabbling with alcoholism; I bonded with Polly.

I came to find that when I was soaking my mind in spirits, Polly was rendered much less annoying. As my state worsened, she became amusing. To my glassy eyes, she seemed to morph again and started to look mildly appealing. Eventually, I found every aspect of her wretchedness attractive. This attraction was, of course, nothing that would conform to the traditional sense of one human being pulled toward another. It was her repulsiveness, and the way she wore it so unashamedly, that hooked me. She had found a way to disintegrate down to the vilest form of trash and then revel in her achievement.

In our common states of delinquency and sloth, we passed the time by pranking one another. When she was in the clutches of a dope hallucination, I would play along and pretend to see the things that she was seeing. Most of the time this frightened her, and I relished the ability to terrorize her with minimal effort. I also liked to hide her rigs and then play a twisted game of *hot and cold* with her as she searched. She would turn the house over in a frenzy, and her rage swelled with every *getting colder* that I uttered. But what could she do? She was a slave to her addiction and I was the keeper of the fix. I took to calling her my Polly puppet. Naturally, she hated the name, but every time I excitedly said *red hot*, I became god.

If I was off my ass and staggering about, she liked to bump into me to see how many objects she could break with my inevitable descent to the floor. Being Polly, these weren't your childish shenanigans. She knocked me through tables, into buckets of piss, and, when they were lit, she delighted in sending me tumbling into the propane heaters. One winter, she switched up her tack and sent me through the ice of our rooftop kiddie pool. She topped off my sobering shock by spraying me down with a fire extinguisher. On more than one occasion, she hip-checked me out a window. This one overlooked the flat roof of the adjoining building. The rubber surface was cracked and the plywood below was soft, but I never fell all the way through, much to the chagrin of my little junk puppet.

The joys we found in our prickly game of reciprocity did the unthinkable, but the inevitable: they brought us together. But the thrills eventually grew stale. We packed away our antics like an old board game that had lost its appeal. Slowly, we began to forget to torture one another. Days went on, then weeks passed. After a time, we just stopped fucking with each other altogether. We never called no truce or decided that enough was enough. We just got bored. After that was gone, well, we were just two people left with nothing but the option of the other's company.

Wayne and Bill were around, sure, but they had distanced themselves from us considerably. I can't rightly blame them. Being sick most of the time from dope and drink, Polly and me liked to sneak up on they fellas as the slept and vomit on them. We really indulged disgust at those times, too. We went about, not just gagging ourselves, but we took turns jamming our fingers down each other's throats. It was a rancid and messy affair, but we thought it was quite the hilarity. Bill and Wayne didn't seem to find the humor in it. I guess showering off junkie ejections with a spray bottle, in the winter, in a house with no heat, just ain't no fun.

Fuck 'em, though. That was our thought process, and not just as it pertained to the Xbox burnouts that, amazingly, continued to share space with us. No, our motto was fit to apply to the whole of mankind. Me and Polly, we was alone, and alone we would always be. It just so happened that, for a spell, we decided to be alone together.

It's safe to say that Polly and me hated each other. A mutual distain was the foundation that supported the temple of decay that was our relationship. But it was in this hatred that we came to respect each other. Like cannibals, we fed off one another. Her ferocity fueled my rage and my violence aroused her ruthlessness. On junk and piss, though, we would never reach the full potential of our barbarism. We both wanted to kick our respective habits. This wasn't in an effort to better ourselves.

No, we realized that in order to be as horrible as our natures would allow, we needed the full spectrum of our senses.

Like any slog out of the wilderness of addiction, gettin' clean proved a trying task. I think we both put in a half-assed effort, but even this lackadaisical approach to sobriety proved beneficial. With less intake, we both became more and more unpleasant. This killed the fun, and knotted resentment into our already gnarled bond. We wanted less to do with each other and, as a result, we both lost our junk buddies. Getting torn to shreds by chemicals just ain't as fun with no one around to impress or piss off.

I was having an easier go putting down the bottle than Polly was having laying low the needle. Drinking, at times, was fun for me. Alcohol is addicting, but fun ain't. It's nice to have around, but it never feels necessary. Fun or no fun, life goes on. Besides, misery is always waiting to move in, and misery proves a much more reliable tenant.

For Polly, though, shooting up was purely medicinal. It was a way for her to shield her mind from the pain. In time, she learned what every user is forced to realize: there ain't no such thing as a user, only the used. By the time dope was done with her, it had exposed all the anguish it was once employed to hide. During a dark night filled with revelation, Polly's affair with narcotics came to an abrupt end.

It was fall, if I remember right. The house was cool. Wayne and Bill had fucked off to parts unknown. It was just me, Polly, and the starlight that cascaded through the windows and spied down through the gaps in the roof. I had a mild buzz going. It made me just calm enough to be tolerant and too lazy to be cruel. Polly, conversely, was ripped out of her head on smack. It wasn't like her to get to talking in such a state. Nodding off and drooling were the activities she normally engaged in after such a heavy shot. But, this night was different. Somehow, her mind fought off the hammers of unconsciousness.

"You know why I do this?" Polly asked, as she waved an exhausted needle in the air.

"Because you're a junkie?" I asked, sarcastically.

"Nope. Wrong as usual, fuckface. I do this because I hate what lives in here." Polly's words might have been slow and slurred, but she had lightning in her hands as she repeatedly jammed her index finger into the side of her head.

"I'm so sick, Kellen," she went on. "I can't forget everything they done to me. I was just a little girl, and all those motherfuckers, they didn't care. Nobody cared. No one ever helped me. Why'd they all think I was so worthless?"

I didn't know the particulars. Hell, I really didn't have much of an idea of what Polly was talking about, but I didn't ask. I felt that if I broke her mutterings, she would shut up altogether. It wasn't compassion that kept me quiet, just curiosity. I wanted to know how much sorrow the junk was capable of wringing from her.

"I ain't worthless!" she insisted. "Or, well, I wasn't anyway. I never wanted any of this. It's just so hard, you know? I mean, I got all this history and shit, and so I do all these things to try and cover it up, and it just makes it all worse."

Polly began to sniffle, and then I saw something that truly shocked me. Polly had tears in her eyes. I didn't see one slip, but she was hurting. This was genuine pain. It was sadness unmasked. Up until that point, I didn't think any emotions at all took residence inside her.

"Like what? What kinda shit do you do?" I asked.

She scoffed and then said, "Don't be an idiot, you know what I'm like. And you know I'm not talking about the drugs. That shit's easy. It's all the other stuff. It comes easy to you, I guess. Hurting people, being an asshole. I don't like doing that, but I don't know how else to be. It's all I know." And then, after a pause, she said, "Why'd it have to be this way?"

She dragged her fingers through her hair and pulled those yellow spikes into ever-sharper points. Polly pulled until a few strands let loose from her scalp. After a few more gave way, she went about banging the backs of her hands against her forehead. She slapped her face, and muted expletives were ground out from between her teeth. And then it came, the deluge.

Her body wrenched forward like she had been hit with a demolition ball. She was on her knees, and by the time her palms slapped down onto the dirty floor, a torrent of tears erupted from her eyes. She snarled and spit. Little shots of puke were rifled out of her mouth and her body shook. I could see the sweat as it oozed out of her and soaked her clothing.

That girl had a force of will in her the likes of which I had never seen. Her determination charged through the affliction that gripped her. She steadied herself and settled her breathing like that of a beast as it attempts to calm itself after a kill. She picked up her head and glared at me. Instinctively, I looked away. I knew then the fear that Bill and Wayne felt when in Polly's presence. There was something in that look that was most unsettling and, as I glanced back at her, I went to rise.

"Why doesn't anyone love me?!" she screamed.

Frantically, Polly continued to cry this sad refrain. Her eyes rolled back into her head, but she just kept at it. Even as her body went into convulsions, she managed to query the whole of the cosmos as to why she was made to suffer such a dearth of affection. It was at this time that I took my leave of her. I went off into the darker spaces of the house, making my way for the roof. Along my path and all throughout the house, her tortured screams rung off the walls and cut the wind as they chased me down. This voice, ghostly and disembodied, seemed to fill the entirety of the world I knew. Even for a misanthrope such as myself, her wails were difficult to absorb. But, among the agony, there was a declaration in her discordant song that was aimed at me, and it was one that I was loathe to acknowledge; my little Polly puppet was cutting her strings.

4. The Prophets Of Atrocity

The winter did come and then it went. All during that time, Polly didn't say word one to me or anyone else. She shot an occasional glance over to the other fellas, but me, Polly couldn't bring herself to look at me. She stalked the hallways and the streets around our place like a specter. It got me to thinking that maybe the junk had taken her that night and what remained was the ghost of a dead girl.

I might have been able to talk myself into the theory of Polly being removed from mortality, but she was very much alive. This tragic fact was illuminated by the horrors she was made to endure as she kicked smack. She hadn't used, not one taste, since that night she fell to pieces before me. I recognized that she viewed that meltdown into abject vulnerability as her ultimate failure. The drugs made her weak in the company of others. To continue to use intoxicants only meant the promise of future emotional frailty. She knew that to fortify her armor, the needle had to go. Still, this don't make shaking junk any easier.

As she combated the urges and ills that withdrawal tends to deal out, Polly displayed the iron nerve of an ibex. The sickness that churned within her was ferocious, but if it did not wield the weapons required to kill her, then Polly was gonna win. She knew it, too, as sure as a nail knows its place under the hammer. The rest of us, we saw it, too. A transformation was taking place inside her. The expected changes came first. Her color returned and her bones regained their ability to hold muscle and meat. Her eyes shed the glaze and her skin healed away all the acne. It was her mind, though, that underwent the greatest mutation.

I clearly remember the day when I saw Polly emerge fully from her personal forest of despair. I was out back of the house with the rest of the guys. Wayne had boosted an old motorcycle and we were taking turns spinning it around in the alley. It was so rickety it might as well have spent the better part of two decades at bottom of the sea. How that tired machine managed to support Wayne's bulk as he went about jumping the curb and bumping into street signs, I'll never know.

None of that is worth a damn and the other activities of the day merit no revisiting. Everything I knew about the world around me seemed to shut down and was sunk into the realm of trivial, inconsequential things as we collectively witnessed Polly step out from the back of the house. The way she looked, having just shed the last remains of her narcotic chrysalis, was a sight to behold. She stood under the light of day a new creature. She walked toward us like a warrior. The more she advanced, the more she took on the mannerisms of a cold machine. She was remade: alive outside, dead within, and more monstrous than ever before.

In order to craft certain explosives a number of different ingredients are required. Without being mixed with other substances, some materials just sit there. Left alone, they are harmless and insignificant. However, when other compounds are introduced, pieces once benign find themselves prone to violence and volatility. Something like that happened to our motley band of losers. The planets aligned and formed themselves into a spear that the four of us would use to hurl at the world.

Polly scrubbed up and got clean. I put the bottle down. This proved fairly easy once I put my mind to the task. I tend to compare my drinking days to those of a mischievous teenager who enjoys starting fires. Things get lit up, and it's fun for a while, but it proves to be just a passing phase. But it weren't just me and the 5'2" bundle of venom that was Polly who underwent changes. No, the others, too, had their turn in the hopper of life-altering events.

Billy boy was wont to do the strange and unexpected. Most of his behavior manifested itself in the form of nervous tics or brief but intense obsessions. He tried his tongue at speaking German for about a week. A taste for the esoteric gripped him and, for a solid month, he spent his days on the roof trying his luck at astral projection. On another occasion, he developed a fondness for action figures. He had no particular preference. Any figure that he could lift from a toy shop or pluck from trash cans suited him fine. He would set them up around the house and stage elaborate situations for his actors to recreate. Naturally, his subjects just sat there with grime on their usually incomplete bodies. This never seemed to phase Bill. Whatever epic scenarios he had envisioned for them all unfolded inside his warped mind. This predilection for random fits of nonsense kept Bill busy and kept him from annoying the rest of us. However, his next fixation would prove long-lasting. Its effects would come to bond the four of us to a destiny yet to be played out in full.

He took a rather fervent fascination with graffiti and the Bible. In among his rummaging for action figures, he had come across an old Bible. With a few flips into the cryptic tome, childish things were cast aside, as his toys no longer held any interest for Bill. Employing various colors of spray paint, he went about applying tags across town.

All the confusion and violence of the Good Book struck Bill's impressionable mind like a God-sized meteorite. By day, he scribbled his favorite quotes over the concrete block of buildings and onto the support columns of underpasses. At night, well, it was Bill's time to shine. While his talent level existed a few leagues down from Michelangelo's, his art rose above the heights of common vandalism. He painted elaborate murals of mystery and monsters. These aerosol sermons must have taken him hours to complete, but, to him, time had disappeared. All that remained was the duty to give fresh praise to the Lord and exalt the wisdom of the Word.

This never made much impression on the rest of us. Wayne seemed disinterested and rather disheartened that his shadow had finally found an identity all its own. In an unprecedented turn of character, I found myself feeling sorry for Wayne. He grew quiet and listless. He knew he had lost a friend and this subtraction cut him deep.

The loss of a friend can be devastating. See, the thing is, friends are a special type of companion. Relatives stick around because, most of the time, they have no other choice. Much the same can be said for spouses, but friends, they are of a different sort. They bond to a person out of choice and hang with them in spite of every variety of flaw and human failure. When they leave, it's simply because they want to, having deemed their former mates no longer worthwhile. That's a hell of a wound to suffer. Every morning Wayne had to drag his ass in front of the mirror and wonder what made him so undesirable. That poor bastard, he wasn't like the rest of us. We were creatures. He was just unfortunate. That loneliness ate him up and, in turn, fate swallowed him whole and spit him back as the perfect pawn for Polly and her schemes.

I simply thought Bill had went insane, not crazy like the rest of us, but legitimately mad. Our little gang might have went about doing things untoward, but that was because we wanted to engage in acts of ill. Which might have been the worst thing about the lot of us. Bill, though, he had a mind sickness, a condition surely exacerbated by living with the human equivalents of bacteria, excrement, and virus.

Polly didn't share my fleeting curiosity as to Bill's latest persona. She was outraged and disgusted by him. This, I could never figure. All his Jesus jive kept him occupied and out of the way. He was rarely around and, when he was home, he didn't go about trying to convert the rest of us. He said that to quote the Bible aloud was blasphemous, as no man is righteous enough to speak the words of the Divine. It was Bill's command, he liked to remind us, to evangelize though images. He viewed himself as a humble interpreter for glory. He would illustrate the path, but it was up to an individual whether or not to walk the road.

As I said, passing curiosities. I found his actions to be lunatic arrogance wrapped up in rags of humility. Most times, his contradictory nonsense gave me a chuckle. In his fervor, he even lost the ability to recognize when he was the target of mockery and scorn. This, of course, made derision a favored pastime for me. He did, however, manage to strike a chord with me on one occasion.

Near the start of his obsession with the Most High, I walked into the house in the early morning hours after a night filled with thievery and imprudence. There, sprayed onto the ceiling, was a quote from Isaiah. I stared at the words that mingled among the cobwebs and cracks. I was immediately pleased, but I quickly found the sentence gravely disturbing. All alone in the dark, I felt something of a fright. It made me shudder. It spoke of the future, and it perfectly articulates my current state.

All my sleep has fled, because of the bitterness of my soul - Isaiah

I gazed up, wide-eyed and wired, at the ominous decoration. I got myself lost in wonder. I can't say for how long I stared and pondered but, in what felt like seconds, the black of night yielded to the dirtied sunbeams of day. Slivers of light snaked into the house and gave away all the dust particles that had previously lain hidden in the empty air. As the words of Isaiah sparkled with the fresh arrival of morning, Polly crept up behind me.

"The fuck is this nonsense?" she said as she rubbed the sleep from her eyes.

I didn't answer. I was mildly startled by her presence. This was the appropriate response when in Polly's company, but it was the way she seemed to materialize out of the dark that jolted me. Normally she clanged around like a freight train whose furnace burned hell fire and atom bombs. There was more to it, though. Her muttered annoyance was the most complete sentence she had voiced in my direction in what had to have been months.

Her lack of communication with me was partly due to my witnessing her dope-driven meltdown into frailty. Mostly, though, Polly had found herself too preoccupied to pay much mind to the rest of us. Shortly after the smack left her system, she hooked up with some chick that stripped at a club a few miles outside of town. This girl, Amy, I think her name was, was a born victim. It was written all over her. She couldn't have tipped the scale over a hundred pounds. She was nervous and skittered around like a rodent. She had dull eyes and a voice that never rose above whispers. I never assumed she was of age, but around the parts we called home, no one cared to investigate such particulars.

Polly and her new pet usually kept to themselves. Where they got off to, I'll never know. But, when I was in their company, I came to notice something strange. Together, they were affectionate, almost tender. I began to think that maybe Amy was gonna crack away at Polly's jagged exterior until the day arrived when the two of them stole off into the night, never to reappear. During the months of their mysterious union, I noted as the two of them shuffled in and out of the house, careful to avoid the rest of us.

I seriously doubt that Amy was ever afraid of me or the other guys. With Polly by her side, I'm sure she felt adequately protected. Polly didn't steer away from us at those times out of embarrassment. That just wasn't her style. This was just misdirection on her part. It was a way to hide the budding authenticity of their relationship. I think the both of them came to feel something which approximated love for one another. Amy, I'm certain, was the obsessive type. Polly, well, I know she would have resisted, but there must have been a tether that kept her close. Polly never allowed herself to display happiness, but when Amy wasn't around, I could see as the glitter fell from Polly's eyes.

After my musing about Polly's wade into the murky waters of intimate companionship, I turned to respond, but stopped when I noticed that she was naked. Her only accessories were a busted lip and a cigarette with bloodstains on the filter.

"What? You never seen titties before?" she asked, and then spat a dollop of blood from her damaged mouth.

"What happened to you?"

"It ain't what happened to me, dude. It's what happened to the other bitch," she said while exhaling smoke.

"We alright now?" I asked.

"Ain't nothing alright, but we can go on like we used to. It was kinda fun. What the hell, anyway. You're better looking than that fat fuck, and not nearly as stupid as Bill. So, yeah, we're okay," she said.

"Where's, um, what's-her-name?" I asked, as I elected not to call Amy by name.

"Now who do you think the other bitch was?" she replied with what would be the last words she would ever speak about Amy. "Hey," she continued, "You want a piece?"

Polly spread her arms out, extending to me the offer of cold and lifeless sex. Her image was that of a snare, a trap stretched open and ready to snap shut over a careless trespasser. I didn't say anything, but she must have seen as intrigue filled my stare.

"Too bad. I'm going back to bed," she said as she turned away. She punctuated my rejection by flicking her cigarette to the floor.

After that, things more or less fell into place. When the days were quiet and lazy, Wayne sulked, Bill continued to spiral into oblivion, and me and Polly bummed around aimlessly. Our relationship became the inverse of the young-love unions as they are represented in films about the 1950s. We mugged the meek and the unsuspecting. We pulled our dinners from trash cans. We stole cars but we never had no direction. Often times, we'd crash the vehicles miles from home, simply because we had grown bored and wanted a brief flash of excitement. Another could always be commandeered for the return trip, anyhow. We had sex only when no other activity was on offer. We rarely showered. We played the parts of pigs and reveled in our collective filth.

When the four of us did come together as one, we lit it up. Our band of miscreants roamed the streets like dogs and terrorized anyone that wandered into our path. Working as a pack, we were able to secure bigger scores. The battles we engaged in won us more desirable spoils. We kept ourselves entertained by paying hobos to drink their own piss. Summarily, we beat the money back out of them and had a laugh with blood on our knuckles. We got better at stealing food, real food. We lit trash fires and rolled the barrels down alleyways and through the windows of storefronts. Anarchy was all that mattered to us. We became the world's most authentic punk band. We lived for lawlessness, never bothering with the comparatively peaceful act of making a record.

But all the crime added up to nothing. It was always the same old shakedown shit. Being bad grew tiresome as we were made to accept, time and time again, that all our deleterious efforts were for naught. Whatever we managed to scrape up or steal was wasted away by the next morning. If we were capable of idolizing anyone, it would have been the gangsters and tyrants of the past, but we were just insects. Our brand of horror only affected the already horrible and didn't reverberate out to the larger world. We were just ordinary thugs. Useless. Worthless. Imminently forgettable. The craving for real destruction bit at all of us, but we was too damn dumb to go about turning the corner from vandal to villain. However, that all changed on the day of revelation.

The day in question came during the cruelest days of August. I woke to the rising of the sun. It ascended like a mushroom cloud. Proud and terrible, it hung in the sky like a globular, congealed mass of the end times. The rays shot down through a thick blanket of humidity and, together, these forces set about turning our corner of the world into an infernal wasteland.

Laid out on the kitchen floor, I was cocooned in a sheet. I peeled away the soiled cloth, unaware of which stains were old and which ones had been deposited from my body the night prior. Unconcerned for the condition of our shared hovel, I cracked open a jug of water and poured it down my throat and about my head and neck. The liquid ran down me and onto the floor. I swear I could hear it sizzle as it pooled over the linoleum.

I staggered out back. The air I sucked into my lungs was harsh and choked with allergens, but at least it moved. I lit a smoke and, carelessly, I tread barefoot onto the asphalt. The ground pressed against my feet like it was made of broken teeth and molten nails. With the flesh of my feet newly damaged, I retreated to the shadows. Situating myself on an upturned milk crate, I glanced down the alley.

Wayne was standing in the middle of the street near the rear exit of an abandoned diner. He was slack-jawed and rigid. I wouldn't have given much of a thought as to what had captivated him so, but his posture was more than just awed stillness. He stood statuesque and possessed. Now, I couldn't rightly image how a dirty old wall of dull bricks and chipped mortar could be the source of such rapt fascination. Discarding my cigarette, I strode over to investigate.

As I drew closer to his position, I noticed Bill. Near the curb, he was set on his knees. His arms were spread wide, his palms turned up to the sky. Slowly, like a scared child might do, he folded his arms tight against his chest. His hands cupped his face and his fingers crawled into the tangles of his dirty hair. I heard as he wept. This was no ordinary crying, no tearful reflex to pain, this was something altogether different. He was bound in the clutches of rapture. An experience beyond the realms of sensible men was having its way with him.

"Hey, what's his deal? Did he miss out on The Feast of the Tabernacle or something?" I shouted over to Wayne.

"No, Kellen, no. You shouldn't joke about these things, Kellen. Serious things. These are serious things," said Wayne.

At first, he seemed to be speaking to me, but as his vague explanation went on, he seemed to be talking more to himself. Or maybe that wasn't quite right. It was almost as though Wayne was addressing the cosmos, calling attention to the good works being done by his wayward friend.

As I approached closer to my entranced housemates, the curiosity I felt nearly eclipsed the discomfort offered by the blaze of morning sun. Once I came upon them, I recoiled at the stench of old fryer grease as it was given a fresh offensiveness from the heat of the day. I gagged a bit and caught a glimpse of rat droppings scattered around the ground. The scraps had long gone away, but the vermin continued to return. Their plight was much the same as ours, I suppose. But, after my nose found a toleration for the stink and my thoughts left the activities of rodents, I gazed up at the wall.

I imagine my reaction mirrored that of Wayne's. I marveled at what Bill had done using nothing more than spray paint and poisoned imagination. The artistry of it, the mastery of craft, flooded me with true appreciation. I was never one to stare wondrously at a work of art, but I could not direct my eyes away from what Bill had done. It was terrible and magnificent. It was frightening and inspirational. It was what we all needed. It was what we had been waiting and longing to experience. It would be the catalyst for our galvanization. We would no more be four separate misanthropes, but a united force for mayhem and evil.

"Polly," I shouted. "Polly, get down here!"

I called and called. I knew she heard me and I knew she was doing her best to ignore my lunacy. She answered to no one and moved under no persuasion but her own, but I was insistent. I'd howl my throat raw if that's what it took to draw her down from the house.

"What the fuck do you want?!" she asked as she appeared on the roof of our building.

"You need to see this," I said.

"See this," she replied and shot me the finger.

Eventually, she popped out into the street. She wore flip-flops, panties, and nothing more. I watched as she aggressively sucked back a few drags from a cigarette and then saw as she extinguished the butt across her left breast. She had fire in her eyes and a rusty steak knife in her hand. She was having a *blood day*. That was a term I took to using to describe the most violent of the moods that enveloped her on occasion. It was the irresistible urge to harm and violate. I had no fear of being stuck, though. I didn't even keep my eyes on her as she came toward us. What I was seeing, what Bill had done, I knew it had the power to quell Polly's fury. Once she stood beside me, I heard as her knife slipped from her fingers and clattered off the ground below.

Bill had channeled Rembrandt and the gutter in equal measure. The mural he created spanned every inch of twenty feet and rose up to the second-story windows of the building. His mind had been cracked open and out had spilled all the color and mysticism of his favorite book. There before our perplexed eyes stood The Four Horsemen of the Apocalypse. This was no daft cartoon based on recycled Bible passages, this was something altogether new. Atop the steeds of damnation, the four of us did ride.

Bill's interpretation of himself was ominous and difficult to ponder. The skin of his shriveled likeness was of an ill pallor. It was lined by veins and pock-marked with sores and old scars. Blood dripped from his eyes, and his opened mouth was all but devoid of teeth. His hair was wild and matted. Bandages wrapped his body, a tattered robe his only proper garment. He rode a black horse that seemed ready to spring forth from the bricks and the fiction and into reality. The beast was sleek and heavily muscled. It contained all the mobility and vigor that Bill had curiously kept from himself. He was a thin man, true, but the choice to associate his two-dimensional self with famine felt grossly masochistic. It made me realize that our artist was no madman. He was sick, and he knew it.

Wayne had been given the white horse of pestilence. It was a ragged animal which appeared to sag under its rider's considerable bulk. Ribs shown through the horse's skin. Its eyes drooped, and portions of its coat had been taken by the influence of malady. In this recreation, Wayne had been fattened up considerably. It was almost as though Bill used part of this masterpiece to articulate what disease had come to mean in modern America. The clothes of pestilence's master were stretched thin and stained by runs of sweat and other bodily excretions. Flies buzzed about nag and man alike. A smattering of indiscriminate filth had been applied over the pair. Dribbles of vomit ran from Wayne's mouth and darkened the areas over which it fell.

Placed on the back of the blood-red horse of war rode my

likeness. My mount was rearing back, with eyes aflame. Hot breath visibly escaping the nostrils. Its hooves shined like polished iron, black tattoos coursed over its skin, and it wore spiked gauntlets over its neck and legs. I was rendered bare-chested and chiseled. My hands gripped weapons of bent rebar and lengths of chain. My hair had been slicked back and lacquered to a heavy shine. It topped my head like a skull cap. My face was twisted into an expression of primal savagery. It was the accurate reflection of the animosity that churned within me. It was the darkest aspects of my temper laid bare and brought to the light of day. It was the face I always hoped to present to the world, my aspiration, me represented at my most tyrannical. My recreator saw fit to grace me with all the power I sought and relieve me of all the weakness I loathed. It was ideal. In perfection, I had been remade.

My eyes then drifted to the centerpiece of Bill's great work: the pale horse of death. Unlike the other steeds, it stood calmly, all four of its hooves resting gently on the ground. The beast had no need to exhibit menace or inspire dread with its posture, for its commander liberally wielded the heaviest of man's fears.

Atop the vehicle of death, Polly had been rendered riding side-saddle. She was draped in a hooded robe of black. It lay open down the center. Over the flesh of Polly's chest, Bill painted a great cavity. It was a gaping abyss where her heart no longer resided. She sat with her legs crossed and each was covered up to the knee in spiked boots. Rivulets of blood dripped from the points and ground-up flesh was stuck to the soles. One hand lay in her lap while the other easily held a buck knife. It was large, serrated, and rusty. Using artistic license, Bill had chosen to swap out the customary scythe for a blade used solely for gutting. There seemed a vulgarity to such a choice, and it suited Polly's brutal nature.

For as threatening as the entire mural was, the greatest care was taken to illustrate the pure horror of Polly. The fine details used to create her expression were the masterpiece inside the masterpiece. Her lips were parted, bent into a crooked smile.

Her teeth had been shaped into points and they appeared to extend from the lacquer in their lust to devour. Her eyes initially seemed obscured by the shadows cast by the hood but, upon closer inspection, her sockets held nothing but empty space. Her stare was hollow. It was darkness incarnate. She had been cast as our champion, the final and absolute authority. The painting was more than illusionary practice, more than an amalgamation of elaborate graffiti and grandiosity run wild, it was truth. Polly was death.

The background of the piece was polluted with fires. Coils of gray smoke ran through the more vibrant oils like snakes as they dip and reappear from water. Crushed under the advance of the horses' hooves were skulls and broken bones. A banner arched over the totality of the work. It looked more like a battle flag. In a jagged script, it read *The Prophets of Atrocity*. I found it interesting that Bill had chosen to shy away from outright branding us as The Four Horsemen. To refer to us as prophets was something else entirely. It meant something else, something more.

The inspiration and future purpose of the work was clear; the four of us were being called to action. We liked to go about masquerading as villains. We fancied ourselves badasses. We were so full of shit. Bill was laying out the challenge. The time had come for us to terrorize or to shut up, shower, and slip into the mediocrity of common existence. I already knew which way we were headed.

At about the time that our collective reveling began to cool, I turned my attention back to the artist. He was still on the ground, still bawling like a child. Tears ran down his face and sweat had soaked through his clothing. It was so goddamned hot, kinda like the fires in Bill's picture added heat to the day, but still he shivered. I looked into his eyes and saw that he was there yet not there. Not anywhere. He had gone somewhere deep, somewhere scary that most of us will never traverse. I noticed as he muttered, and knelt down for a listen.

"It is done. They have seen it, my work, your command,"

Bill said shakily. "We are the riders, the fury and the storm. All shall know your power and your will. We will carry on our tongues and on our swords the truth of glory, death, and God. God, glory, and death. Death, God, and glory. Death to the God of glory, glory to the God of death…" he went on, bending the words into different patterns and murkier meanings.

Bill had gotten stuck in some anguished mental loop. He was probably going to carry on like that for the better half of the day. None of us elected to lend further time to his lunatic rantings, but I think we all absorbed the point. One by one, we peeled off and left him to the insanity and baking asphalt. We shuffled back to the house, unsure of what really to do next. I don't recall much of anything that went on the rest of that day, or even the rest of the week. But, like some ancient prophecy, it all came together soon enough.

5. Lights Out

Things started off slow and a little clumsy. We fell back into the old habits of engaging in street-level violence and random acts of cruelty. We was all changed, though, and knew that a higher responsibility to chaos had been forced onto us. The funny thing was, Bill never went into detail about the events of the day that led him to paint away well into the dark hours of night. None of us pressed him for meaning, either. I don't think the specifics much mattered to any of us. What did seem to resonate was that Bill had assigned us roles that made each of us comfortable.

Polly had been cast as the leader. We needed her drive, her willingness to cross every line of basic decency. Wayne became our mascot. He reminded us of what we were and did as he was told. I became the hammer. Polly would point and I'd swing, just happy to have something to smash. As for Bill, outside of being an inspiration for madness, he was mostly useless and remained a liability. None of that mattered. We were the creatures that we were, convenience and complications be damned. I think what Bill had done was allow the rest of us to accept ourselves. We no longer needed to justify our behavior or feel guilty for the messes we made. Not everyone can move in the light. Some need to exist in the dark. Why shouldn't it be us?

With our enthusiasm for crime and carnage renewed, we hit the road. Together we had managed to get an abandoned van back into running shape. It wouldn't last for long, but it would serve our purpose. Our path took us around the eastern parts of the Upper Midwest. Once known, our presence would be unwelcome wherever the van took us, but we pulled off some big hits during our tour.

Riding together, crammed into an uncomfortable and filthy vehicle, felt invigorating. We were actually doing something. What transpired weren't never going to be good, but it was going to leave a mark. A stain. Like proper travelers, we played road games. Counting personalized license plates and punching each other over Volkswagen Bugs didn't factor in, though. As the miles clicked off, we kept ourselves entertained in the only ways we knew how, by being gross and lawless.

Taking turns at the wheel, we awarded ourselves points for intentionally driving over roadkill. Hitting a live animal scored a big bonus, though we did take some logical precautions and took the van's health into consideration if a deer came into view. We delighted in taking the mirrors off of parked cars with ball bats. Me and the fellas would shake our dicks at old women and Polly went about flashing her tits at passing truckers. Her peep shows caused a few trucks to swerve, but her indecency never managed to cause a full-on accident. I know that always bothered her.

During stops for gas and theft, we knifed tires and chiseled emblems from cars. Bill had a knack for acquiring Tesla logos. Those cars were still relatively rare back then and so he quickly outshone the rest of us and our pitiful collections of domestic insignias. We scraped up some cash along our path but rarely bothered to rent a room. Instead, we all slept, shit, and fucked in the van. This, of course, meant we had new ammunition for the next run of highway warfare. We dropped bags of excrement over the sides of bridges and flung used condoms out the windows before hurriedly scurrying off an exit ramp.

I don't know if we was charmed and lucky, or if everyone else was just cursed and unfortunate, because we never once got pulled over by the cops. I'm sure our misery machine was called in for random acts of indecency more than once, but punishment never came calling. This only emboldened us. We felt like it was our duty to take this commitment to chaos as far as we possibly could.

We targeted places none of us had visited before, but the environs of ghettos and crippled mill towns always felt familiar. We resurrected the scheme that put Polly into the role of hooker. She would loiter around alleyways while me and the others camped out in the van. Any time she could entice a john out of his car and into the shadows, we set to work. Me and Wayne saw to the beatings while Polly and Bill rifled through the victims' cars. With great success, we ran this ruse to perfection.

I knew the charade was growing stale for Polly, though. She was never no good at sticking to anything for too long. Hell, even dope had become boring for her. One particular night the setup was the same and all the pieces were falling into place. She had hooked a john and me and the boys were set to spring. We rushed into the darkness but Polly was nowhere to be found. Keeping quiet, we stalked around and worked our way deeper down the dead-end street.

I finally caught sight of her under the flickering light of a cheap neon sign. Her palms flat out against a wall, she was bent over and getting done by an old man. Of all nights to commit to method acting, I couldn't figure her reasons. It was cold. Rain was biting down, and a harsh wind had been funneled through the gaps between the buildings. It cut into all of us. With her skimpy top, and with her shorts lying limp around her ankles, she had to be freezing. Her eyes lit up when she noticed me.

She smiled and removed one of her hands from the wall. She made a fist and then raised her middle finger to me. Her gesture hung in the air for what felt minutes.

"Fuck you, Kellen!" she screamed, before breaking into a fit of hysterical laughter.

It was about this time that the old guy got wise that something was amiss. That didn't matter. He was too old for fast reaction and he was spellbound to the fact that he was giving it to a woman approximately forty years his junior. He kept at it, the way a child continues to aimlessly play around with his toys while being admonished by a parent. Ignorance can be bliss, but it ain't never been a shield against punishment.

Polly whipped around and clocked the old pervert in the temple. I don't think she had the strength to knock him out, but he went down anyway. Hiking up her shorts and fixing them in place with a quick shimmy of her hips, she plucked a brick from the ground. Rain dripped off the stone as she raised it, but with the next ascent of her weapon, it would drip blood. She set about bashing his head in, laughing the whole damn while. This wasn't no emanation of joy. The sound that left her mouth was a morbid cackle. The noise was more mechanical than human. I never heard nothing like it. The way it echoed through the alley and scraped off the walls was terrifying.

The rest of us tried to advance. To what end, I don't know. Polly wouldn't allow us to get near her. Anytime we got close, she screamed us away and threw discarded bottles and other garbage in our direction. She wouldn't even let us loot the car. It was a Lexus. Who knows what treasures it held. Polly couldn't be bothered with such trivialities. With her bloodied brick, she took out the passenger window. She pulled an old coat from the backseat, lit it up with a Zippo, and cast it back into the car. After that, we simply walked away and got in the van. A luxury car blazed in the rearview mirror and a man lay dying or already dead a bit further back. None of us behaved as though anything out of the ordinary had taken place.

I guess this was the logical end to the prostitute pantomime hustle. The street pimps were getting wind of our game. They didn't know who we were, but we were marked nonetheless. With word getting around about our working-girl ruse, business had dropped off. The girls that normally worked the corners didn't recognize Polly, but soon enough they put two and two together. It was time for us to move on but, more importantly, it was time for us to raise the stakes.

Reason might suggest that it was the three males that came up with the hooker con. We pushed our small female counterpart into the act, let her take the risks, and we would sweep in to collect the rewards, right? Not so. It was all Polly, every time. She was the leader and we knew better than to question her calls, lest we end up under a brick. After all, we did sleep sometimes.

With us, there was never a need for a powerplay. No one else wanted the responsibility and the think-time required to formulate new deceptions. What can I say? Polly was a mastermind, anyway. She networked and dug up connections with every lowlife and moral monstrosity this side of the Mississippi river.

She got us in the racket of stealing cars and sending them off to be chopped. During one particular drop-off, Polly accepted a sizeable amount of cocaine in lieu of cash. We tried cookin' it up into crack, but none of us knew the technique. That scheme was mostly a bust but, hell, it was something to do. More than anything, I think Polly wanted to test her resolve around such a temptation to use. She never so much as sniffled deeply around the shit. Later, she hooked us up with some guys that worked security at the sleaziest of pawn shops. With the aid of our recruited inside men, we absconded with armfuls of guns and jewels. We took turns shuttling the goods hither and yon to sell them off a safe distance from our territory.

Any time we employed the help of others, Polly made sure they were paid promptly and generously. On our off days, she set up strategy meetings in the van. She always had something else grinding through that monstrous mind of hers. The next score was in her thoughts before the current one could be fully appreciated. And, speaking of which, we raked in tons of cash and rarely did anything with it. I imagine for us, and for Polly specifically, the spoils fell victim to the feeling of the chase being better than the catch.

It's funny for me to think of all this now, because I can't rightly say if any of it was fun. It felt good, all of it, the destruction, the carnage, the violence. But was it fun? I guess not, or maybe I just forgot that part, along with so many other things. I do have a clear memory from that time, however. The memory is of a break in the action, an interlude between the horrors we had already accomplished and the true terrorism we were set to bring.

Sometime after the hooker bait-and-switch fell apart, we hit a stride and had a streak going that featured nothing but good luck and near-misses. The close calls, whether they were from the law or street rivals, just made us feel more invincible. We were on our way back to the house when Wayne suggested that we get a hotel room and have a bit of a celebration. This wasn't the type of thing we usually did. Business was business. Screwing off and getting drunk in hotel rooms was for amateurs. But, on that night, it all felt right.

We checked into a moderately tolerable roadside dive. Polly headed straight for the shower, while me and the others unloaded the spoils from the van. Once in the room, we spread out the bounty over the lone bed and marveled at our success. But the strangest part? Not much of anything happened after that. The four of us were relatively calm, model tenants, I imagine, compared to the lot that the inn was accustomed to hosting. There was no drinking, no drugs. No one had sex with Polly, and no one threw up on the floor. We didn't lure an unsuspecting victim in to harass and violate. For once, we conducted ourselves like humans.

This quiet night doesn't seem the sort of thing that would occupy space in the mind and, for a while, I wondered why it did. Years later, I came to realize why this memory has stuck with me. It was for the small things. It was for all the things we didn't do. We sat around each other watching TV and telling jokes into the quiet hours of the morning. We behaved like friends, common people happy just to share the company of each other. Now, I know that none of us, besides Wayne, maybe, ever put much value on what it meant to have a friend. But we all seemed to be made calm, almost content, by the experience. I remember Bill coming down from the clouds and speaking to Wayne like he once did when they shared an affinity for video games on the couch. I can still see the soft light of the television as it brightened Polly's face. I recall how innocent she sounded as she laughed at the cartoons on the screen. I remember feeling comfortable.

It all could have changed for us then. That night could have been the turn that would set us up to go right. It's a shame that an event such as this proved to be nothing more than an aberration. For a brief moment, we saw what it meant to be better, to be normal, and still we elected to continue on in the wrong direction. I get it, now, that our single night of equanimity was the true beginning of the end. It wasn't put plainly, but subconsciously I think we all recognized that we were honestly deplorable. Nature and misfortune didn't hammer us into the darkened spaces we occupied. We chose to exist there. That's what made us all so terrible. Somewhere along the way, we had opted to shed our basic humanity and adopt the nature of beasts. I think about that every day. It makes me wonder, why the hell did we seem so surprised when it got worse?

All of our previous mayhem paled in comparison to the next angle we decided to work. We had reservations, and skepticism was voiced, but eventually Polly talked us into doing home invasions. It was bold work, often sloppy, always violent. People were hurt, children were made to cry, and pets got killed. Things were getting out of hand, and it was all getting a bit much to take. During these acts of barbarism, Bill took to assuming the role of spectator, although he occasionally would read aloud from the Book. It's now disturbing to remember how his recitation of God's word only served to heighten the horror. I enjoyed the chaos and found great satisfaction preforming my duties as enforcer and barking orders to Wayne. But it wasn't that simple. It was the collateral damage that began to wear on me.

Now, I ain't trying to say that I was going soft or that something of a conscience was blooming within me. I am a bad man. I am an abhorrent man. Never doubt the nature of a disease, for it will not change. But I was tiring of the game all the same. It was the harming and terrorization of children that got to me. I always found kids to be insufferable brats, but there is innocence in children. Not all, but some, and during the whirlwind of a home invasion, it's impossible to tell who's already poisoned and who's truly innocent. In the faces of those kids, I saw a change happening. I saw all the dirty things that conspired to make me what I was, and what I am again.

Now, I know I said that I do the things I do out of choice. That still holds true. But don't underestimate the influence that traumatic events and the toxicity of environment can have on a person, especially a child. It all got too much to bear once the eyes of those kids started to look like mirrors. I do not like me. I do not desire to see replications of myself in others. Creatures like me are to be disposed of and despised. The fewer of us there are, the better.

When Wayne noticed my displeasure and lack of enthusiasm, he felt emboldened to speak out against Polly's latest favorite activity. He tried to work around the real issues by complaining about the masks Polly made us wear. She liked to pick out cute masks, like cartoon characters or pop stars. She said it amped up the fear factor for our victims. She wasn't having any of Wayne's protestations and basically blew him off. Next, he pulled the jail card. He ranted and raved about how it was only a matter of time before we were caught and locked up. This was a legitimate concern, but Polly simply didn't care. To her, worrying about prison was for pussies. She told him to man up and accept the end in whatever form it would take. The freight train of destruction was gonna continue to hammer down the tracks, end of story.

Our dear leader had found a new high. It made her giddy. This led to irrationality and greed. It all had to end sometime and, quicker than any of us would have guessed, it did. Polly was setting up checkmate. She recognized that a threat had come to the playing board and so she laser focused on its elimination. She dressed up her move as the next big score, the biggest one yet. She promised it would satisfy everyone, and we were all dumb enough to swallow the lie.

During the early hours of an evening in spring, me, Wayne, and Bill were just kicking it on the couch. We were in front of the TV, enjoying the crisp graphics of our recently ill-gotten PS4. Some scented candles were burning. They were one of the small luxuries we allowed ourselves. Even this was more necessity than indulgence. With the warmer months approaching, our house was set to smell more rancid than usual, so it was nice to have some Sunshine Breeze mingle among the stale air.

I think the three of us were all hoping for a quiet night, but the crusader, who was still asleep, would pay no never mind to the desires of her underlings. Right about the time that Wayne and myself were laying waste to hordes of zombie orcs, Polly came bouncing down the stairs. She was dressed neatly and somewhat conservatively, by her standards. She was fresh-faced and dolled up like she was ready for the first day of senior year. Her attitude was light. She was goddamned effervescent. So much energy seemed to be rattling around inside of her, I was surprised when she plunked down in a chair. She fired up a cigarette, the side dish to her meal of juice and Cheetos, and eyed us eagerly.

"Listen up, my minions!" she said. "I've got the big one all worked out. This, this is going to be fucking huge. After this, we can get out of this hellhole, go somewhere warm, and spend all this fucking cash!" Like a cheap magician, she produced two fistfuls of money and waved them in our direction.

We turned to face her, but with little excitement. She had taken a fancy for calling us her minions, which I found rather annoying. Wayne seemed to find it cute and endearing, while Bill saw it for what it really was; condescending. Anyway, we knew it best to give the squeaky wheel the grease. Besides, without our prompt attention, she would take a hammer to the PS4, so we thought it more diplomatic to just save our game and see what was on her mind.

I could never picture Polly as a bubbly teenager. I always assumed she had skipped that phase, going straight from womb to witch. But she went on about her plan with all the spirit of a high school cheerleader. Apparently, she had arranged for us to meet with a fairly high-end drug dealer that operated in the general area. His name was known to me, and Polly seemed to know all the particulars about our prospective deal. None of it was made to sound dangerous, or even risky. This was purely business and the meet would demand our collective professionalism.

She was selling us a dream. Well, maybe it was just me she had to sell, but I was the only one she needed. She promised that this score would free us from the constraints suffered by the common thug. It was time to move up, to take our rightful share of the big time from the underworld. It was our destiny. As she went on about fate, Bill became visibly enthralled. I think he got lost in the deception. Even I was beginning to buy it. I certainly had misgivings about going corporate. It didn't suit me. I liked the grime and the scum. If I would have considered the proposal more clearly, I would have realized that it didn't suit any of us.

Wayne dressed up his anxiety with giddy laughter. He nudged me as Polly spoke and I felt my face as it cracked into a smile. They really had me going. The pitch pulled me in and, once I was snared, there was no going back. Long before I realized it myself, Polly saw the genuine zing in my eyes. It was then that she moved the final pieces into play.

"Okay, here's the thing," she began. "We can't show up looking like we normally do. This dude plays with the pros, so we can't look like scum fucks. There's no way he'd take us seriously. So how about you three homos clean yourselves up, put on whatever you have that ain't filthy, and be in the fucking van by ten. Hey, shit, I'm starving. I'm gonna run down to the Sunoco and stuff my face with donuts. I think I'll even pay for 'em, too! We play it straight today, no fucking around. C'mon, losers. Chop, chop!" she said as she clapped her hands together and bounded up out of the chair.

I couldn't figure the situation. It was so matter-of-fact, and it sounded to me like actual work. I still don't know why I ascended the stairs and readied myself for the shower. Maybe it all came down to the comfortable reality that there was a functional shower for me to enjoy. It was a while back that Bill had tracked down the rightful owner of the property we occupied. I don't know the specifics of the deal but, as it happened, the deed holder was trash like us. So before I knew it, we had running water. It was still cold, but it provided proper cleansing all the same. I stepped into the tub, careful to avoid the more jagged cracks in the porcelain, and cranked the valves open.

With all the splashing and my own gasping born from the sting of cold water, sound came to me filtered and fuzzy. I was sure I had heard the van start, though. It was an unmistakable squeal, a howl that spoke to its age and abuse. I pondered on it for a second. I began to think that the others viewed me as too brutish for the meeting and had elected to leave me behind. And that's when it hit me. Not some ephemeral notion of enlightenment, but the tank lid from the toilet.

I had no time to react. Wayne, I imagine, was the one who tackled me to the floor and enveloped me in the shower curtain. Polly, certainly, was the one who delivered the blow. Before I slipped unconscious, I heard a cacophony of frantic voices. I heard as Bill went about preaching. In my state, I couldn't arrange the words properly, but his excited delivery escalated into ever more ominous tones. Wayne's voice wove in and out of the noise, and I pieced together its meaning. He kept seeking reassurance and praise from Polly. I suspect he didn't like what he had found himself a part of, and so he constantly sought out moral support and justification from his master. And then there was that inhuman laughter. It was the same wretched din I had absorbed when Polly took to beating down the old john. Hearing that, I knew it was over for me. I was done. There was no coming back from this.

I had a moment of clarity right before the end. There never was no meeting. No deal. No need to be fancy, and there sure as hell weren't no fucking donuts. The plan that Polly had put forth sounded ridiculous and phony because that's exactly what it was. She had schemed up a way to be rid of me and had the others in on it long before they attacked me in the bathroom. And to think, as I sat on that couch next to those two bastards, my fate was already sealed.

What happened next wasn't made known to me until much later. But, apparently, this is how the end, or rather, the hibernation of Kellen Black went down. With my lights knocked out, I was dragged down the stairs and loaded into the van. With Polly at the wheel, they sped off toward a stretch of rural highway that arched over the interstate. Among the dusk of the evening, I was dumped out onto the road. And then they waited. This was the part of the plan that was actually brilliant. From the overpass, the three of them kept a sharp eye on the traffic below. They were looking for something in particular, and waiting for just the right moment.

All this standing around by the side of the road with a lifeless body sure must have made them nervous. I like to think about the arguing and screaming that must have taken place as the anxiety ate away at their nerve. I'm sure this task revealed to them how desperate and weak they all truly were. Polly saw this move as removing a threat to her authority, but it would prove to fracture whatever hold she still had over Wayne and Bill. They all had to feel it, even Polly, for not long after my disposal, they would split off in different directions. But what did that matter? They were still gonna finish one last job together, and that job was me.

A lone tractor-trailer came into view. It was the opportunity they had so eagerly awaited. I was hoisted up onto the barrier, and right before the truck slipped under the pass, I was tossed over. Just as Polly had envisioned, I collided with the roof of the trailer, broke through the fiberglass top, and was carried off into the dark to parts distant and unknown with the rest of the cargo.

Like most things, it took years for this memory to return to me. Even now, this event exists in my mind in fragments. Over time I've been able to assemble the pieces into something of a cohesive order. The picture remains incomplete and the recollection is fuzzy, but it's there.

The sensation that has stuck with me the most wasn't the collision with the roof of the trailer. It is not the vision of the trees as they seemed to uproot and roll over me. It ain't the feel of the rain, or the realization that my value as a human being was seen as no higher than common trash. Nor is it the punishment I suffered as my body crumpled over the cargo. I have a faint recall about such things, but the impression that has never left me is the feeling of weightlessness. During my descent, the seconds elongated themselves into what felt like hours. My body was rocketing toward the earth below but, somehow, I absorbed the experience of what it must feel like to float. This could have been symptomatic of the trauma I had already suffered. Maybe it was my brain shutting down. I can't know for sure, but it felt like so much more. It felt transcendent.

I was thrown, not just from a random overpass, but from the very edge of the world. I was cast adrift from myself. I discovered a sensation of freedom. I felt absolved. Fate saw fit to gift me with the opportunity to disappear and then reemerge as someone new. For decades, I carried on in a state of suspension, but down was always my inevitable destination. I fell from the sky and, though it took twenty years, I finally, and cruelly, came through the clouds and crashed back down to earth.

Chapter Two: The Man Who Fell To Earth

6. Scattered Pieces

"Is there anything you can give us? Do you remember anything about what happened to you? Can you tell me your name?"

"Paul. Uh, my name is Paul…Parker."

That was my best guess. It just kinda came out. I didn't believe, with much certainty anyway, that my name was, in fact, Paul Parker. The words fell out of my mouth like a reflex. I realize now that what I had said was one part reaction, one part explanation. Thing is, my mixed-up mind was trying to explain *what* had happened to me and not *who* I happened to be. It didn't matter. I had nothing else to give. Those who surrounded me took my name as Paul Parker and I had no reason to doubt them. It sounded familiar, and it stuck with me like nothing much else had done. So I became Paul Parker. But, before that, and much the same as anyone else who has been born, a series of fateful events preceded the unlikely existence of Paul Parker.

As a stowaway, unconscious and nearly dead, I was carried in that truck out of Ohio and deeper into the Heartland. Stops were made along the way. My carriage was passed off to another driver, dropped, hooked, and set on down the road again. All the while, I lay folded up among the goods, bleeding and breathing shallowly. Finally, the truck docked, the trailer door was rolled up, and out I tumbled onto a warehouse floor located a few miles outside of Stone Horse, Nebraska.

Naturally, what followed was rather uneventful. I'm sure my arrival brought with it a few fireworks of excitement to the good folks of Custer County, but nothing much really happened. I've been told that I spent the better part of two weeks yo-yoing in and out of consciousness. In the due course of time I came to, but I might as well have stayed under and used that time to snag some extra sleep. Though awake and relatively mobile, my mind and body couldn't offer clues as to who I really was. By some miracle, I had managed to avoid arrest during the first twenty-four years of my life. It should come as no surprise that I had never seen a dentist proper. I had no identification and no memory. Furthermore, no one was looking for me. I was a mystery man.

During my stay in the hospital, I became a puzzle that everyone wanted to put back together. The cops asked me questions, and the newspapers relished the latest riddle to be trucked into town. Wild gossip wove its way through the halls of the hospital. Some took my abrupt appearance and the subsequent enigma to be a sign from powers above. Others saw me as evidence of a clandestine government operation gone wrong. Some particularly kind-hearted folks went about creating a Facebook page dedicated to reuniting me with myself. Mine was just the type of story that held the collective interest of the internet for about a week.

I found myself among the whirlwind. Nobody's sense of confusion ran deeper than mine during those initial weeks. I was anxious to learn of myself. I was scared to discover who I truly had been. I could barely recognize myself in a mirror, but somehow, I remained more afraid of revelation than of the prospect of being forever lost. I had taken one hell of a beating but, still, in the back of my mind, I sensed that the pieces of me scattered out on the road were best left behind.

Years later, I wondered about whether or not Polly and company saw me on the news or caught a glimpse of my story online. If they had, not one of 'em was gonna offer information to shed light onto the curiosity I had become. But that ain't what I thought about anyway. I got to thinking about fear, about the image of three people soaked with sweat and holding their breath. I hoped they saw me and stayed quiet. I hoped they saw me, all dumb and busted up, as the promise of things to come. I like to think that for the last twenty years, each one of them has been glancing over their shoulders and peering under their beds before they go to sleep at night. Oh, I hope that their minds carved away a little time each day to think of me. I have fantasized about how it must needle them, the not knowing, but, also, the knowledge that at any moment I might reappear to destroy them. But after a time, my thinking changed. I took to the sincere hope that they had forgotten me entirely. I started to dream about what it would be like to be there, to collect the debt owed, at the very moment that they all finally decided to exhale. I don't think like that anymore, though.

Once I had stabilized, came to, and healed up the more serious wounds I carried, reality came to call for me. The first stressor that awaited me was with the law. The police don't have much patience for waiting around, so, as soon as I could string together a coherent response to their questions, the questions did come. All their digging was in vain. What little evidence that existed for my present condition had been scattered to the winds. What was worse, the cops were unable to settle on a location that had hosted my fall from the sky. They didn't even have a starting point. With nothing to go on, and with even less coming from me, the frustration mounted. Eventually, their vexation turned into exhaustion, which summarily devolved into disinterest. As time went by, there were other cases to focus on and I didn't seem like that big of a deal. I forgot myself, and, as fate would have it, I found myself forgotten.

My plight, and the burst of intrigue that followed initially gripped the internet and evening news, but such things cool off. The interest falls away, the news cycle pushes on and webpages refresh. Once it looked like a safe bet that I was destined to live the remainder of my existence in the *lost* box, the world moved on to newer mysteries. This is just the natural way of things. I don't bear no grudge against those that gave up on me. After so long, once something misplaced proves itself to be difficult to find, it gets replaced. That's what happened to me and, if I'm honest, there were people far more important that warranted the public's attention.

The next obstacle that I came to face was the task of carving out a new existence. It was explained to me that I was suffering from a form of retrograde amnesia. In the beginning, I needed assistance reacquainting my body with proper movement, and my speech seemed a tick off pace, but I regained such skills fairly quickly. The memory of things past, though, that was what I no longer had. I was told that I might one day recall the prior experiences I had been cut off from, but the likelihood of such a return was truly anyone's guess. Some people in my situation saw their memories flood back en masse. Others experienced this return as a trickle. In some cases, this mental reunion happened in a matter of days. It sometimes took months, years, even. In some instances, it never happened at all.

While in the hospital, I didn't ponder much over the condition of my memory or lack thereof. It was too difficult a task in that environment. Hospitals are places filled with stimuli that the average person is unaccustomed to experiencing. Concentration is a dog too wild to chain in such a place. However, the day was quick to come when I would be forced to move back out into the world. Physically, my convalescence was complete. I was an able-bodied young man. I could communicate. I could work. I could look after myself. I couldn't stay.

I ended up being placed into a halfway house of sorts. It was partially funded by the state, but was mostly propped up by means of charity and kept running with the aid of volunteers. Once upon a time it was probably a beautiful residence but, long before I arrived, that was all gone. The insides were broken up and partitioned off in order to make way for about a dozen tiny apartments. The appliances were old and the wallpaper curled away near the corners and along the baseboards. Portions of the ceiling had yellowed with time and cracks ran through the plaster. The furnace growled angrily and the pipes banged about with every use of a shower or toilet. It really wasn't so nice, but it wasn't too bad either. It was damn sure the nicest place I had ever called home.

Not that I knew it then, but my new housemates were kinda like those with whom I had previously kept company. There were those recovering from junk and drink. A few residents were in the difficult process of making the transition from the mechanical ways of prison life to the chaos of free living. I shared space with those afflicted by various mental handicaps and illnesses. Among the haunted and broken things, I felt an odd sense of familiarity.

These people could live productively and get by, just not without a little supervision and guidance. Everyone there, except me, had something in common: they were kind people. No one there had a violent history. Oftentimes, these folks fell victim to the gullibility brought about by their gentle natures. They were precisely the types I once preyed upon. Why I was slotted in there is a mystery to me. I expect that the vetting process wasn't too thorough. Or, maybe those in charge had a touch of the clairvoyant in them. I had a violent past indeed, but it seemed I would not have a violent future.

I was given a room all to myself. This was rare. Almost everyone there had a roommate. Before my tumble from the overpass, I would have viewed this development favorably. However, I found myself disappointed that the time spent in my room would be time spent alone. I can't quite explain that, but I had a yearning for companionship. I wanted to get to know the others. I was interested in them. I was, dare I say, concerned for them. Maybe the reason for this was that I was a stranger to myself and, as such, I felt the desire to bond with the strangers around me.

I remember my first night there. It was nice to be without the beeps and buzzers of the hospital that had incessantly interrupted the calm of silence. I studied the old television set, and the collection of outdated magazines that rested over the sag of cheap shelving units. I had a twin bed and a dinged-up dorm fridge. My bathroom was small. The shower tiles were cracked and the sink faucet suffered a constant drip. It certainly wasn't much but, for a while, it was mine. I felt safe there. I felt joyous. Before I lay down to sleep, I peered out the lone window of my room. Through the glass, I watched the sun as it dipped down onto the plains. A rural route snaked off into the horizon. Some distance down the road was a house. It wasn't yet 9 o'clock but all the lights were turned out. I spotted an old windmill and watched the blades as they turned lazily with the breeze. There wasn't much else to see but I felt soothed by the minimalism and simplicity of the scene. I stayed there at the window until the sky went dark. Every star in the cosmos seemed to be held over Nebraska that night. I was hesitant to surrender to sleep. I felt happy but also afraid. I was scared that in the morning it might all be gone.

Before too long, I settled in and made a few friends. I passed the time by playing chess with a middle-aged guy that everyone called Dumbo. His real name was Randy, and I suspected he was autistic. Initially, calling him by his nickname seemed to me rather cruel. Turns out he had something of a fascination for the cartoon elephant of the same name. He was the type that depended mightily on routine to maintain balance and, any time stress was getting the better of him, he would take in a few scenes from *Dumbo*. This mild retreat into fantasy straightened him right out. His handle was also of the ironic sort. Randy, it seemed, had crammed all the knowledge of the known universe into his mind. Consequently, I never even came close to giving him a decent match on the game board, but we had fun. I liked to listen to his stories and he enjoyed teaching me things. My plight astonished him and, though I never asked him to do so, he took on the responsibility of giving me an education.

The Three Musketeers candy bar was originally three different flavors: strawberry, chocolate, and vanilla. In the

1970s, Mattel sold a doll whose breasts could be made larger with just a twist of her arm. Earnest Vincent Wright's novel, *Gadsby*, all 50,000 words of it, contains not a single use of the letter e. Some species of snail have over 20,000 teeth. There wasn't much that I learned from Randy that could be applied in any practical sense, but it was nice to learn a little bit more about anything with my every failure at being a competent chess player.

Another man, an ancient fellow named Bernard, usually kept me company into the small hours of the morning. He had spent much of his life in prison for muling drugs and stealing cars. He was gentle, gregarious, and interminably interesting. We'd sit out on the back porch and watch the sun give way to the rise of the moon. He had trouble sleeping and I still had enough youthful energy to get up early and stay up late. He was bald, wore wire-framed glasses, and down his chest cascaded a wiry beard. It grew out like a corkscrew, white underneath, while above, it was traced over by nicotine stains. He smoked his tobacco any way that he could get it and performed simple magic tricks during our talks.

He regaled me with tales of out-running the federales across the deserts of Mexico. With pride, he rattled off the makes of every car he had boosted, and, with joy, he did the same with the names of women he had taken to bed. Amongst his tales of prison breaks, nights spent around casino tables and long days of working laundry duty in the joint, he indulged his fondness for sleight-of-hand. As we spoke, he'd pop golf balls out of his mouth and cause coins to vanish and then reappear. I took to loading down my pockets with whatever I had, just to see how much he could manage to swipe from me while I was lost in his stories. Sure, I didn't believe everything he said, and I saw through most of his tricks, but it was pleasurable to have someone around that wanted to talk to me.

Bernard died not long into my residency there at the house. I didn't know him well. In actuality, I probably didn't know him at all, but his passing hurt me. Everybody there seemed affected by the absence created by the departure of our beloved wizard. Like me, no one else knew much about Bernard, but all grieved his death. He was something of a legend in Stone Horse, and even those that had never met the man took time out to attend his funeral. It was during his service that the old man had one last lesson to give me. Looking out over all those people who turned up to see off a stranger showed me the value and rewards of what affection and charm can bring. Kindness and patience are intangible things. They cannot be measured, but the worth of such practices proves invaluable.

During my stay, I managed to make a third friend which, as it turns out, made for a total of three more than I had collected during the first two decades and change of my life. Her name was Xalbadora, and she was every bit as plain and reserved as her name was illustrious and exotic. I never knew what it was that cut her out of ordinary life and set her among the damaged things. Anxiety had quite a grip on her and the peculiar behaviors associated with obsessive compulsive disorder had their way with her now and again. I imagine she was just another unfortunate soul whose mind was a shish kabob of mental complications.

We didn't seem to have much in common. We didn't trade late-night philosophy or challenge each other's wits around a card table. We never entertained each other with parlor room deceits or stupid human tricks. Sometimes, we didn't even talk. That was just it though, when we was together, we could just sit still and in silence. I never really got to know her but there was a sense of comfort that came attached to the mystery. Around her, I would never be judged and I couldn't go about passing judgment on her. I think she liked me because I wasn't the questioning type. I was happy to have her company simply based on her being a warm, anonymous creature placed in my vicinity.

"Paul," she said to me one night, "I don't think I'm going to be here tomorrow." After this statement she sat back in her chair and turned away. The words that she spoke laid over us like an old fringed coat. There were loose ends dangling down everywhere from what she had said, but Xalbadora acted as though the conversation was over.

"Don't you worry, Xal, you'll be right here in the morning, and tomorrow will be just as boring as today," I replied, trying to sound light.

"No, I don't think so. I'm going away."

"You can't leave. If you go who am I going to have to *not* talk to?" I asked, and she smiled.

"I like you, Paul. You've always been sweet to me. Everybody else just thinks I'm a weirdo. I'll miss you."

"Xal, seriously, what are you going on about?"

"I don't know. It's probably nothing. Would you be willing to sleep in my room tonight? Not *with* me, you know, but could you just be there?" she asked.

Unsure of that she was truly getting at, I nodded, and in short order we were in her room. Her roommate, Sheryl, was a recovering addict. About a week back she tested dirty and was carted off to jail. She might as well have never existed in the first place. In the room in which I stood only one personality was reflected, and it was Xalbadora's.

The room was white and the furniture was sparse. Every object, knick-knack, and article of clothing had a place and a purpose to their placement. But, just like its occupant, the room had secrets hidden below the surface. Xalbadora turned out the lights and asked me to lay down with her. In the dark, and in a low voice, she told me that she had written over every wall in invisible ink. She said her message could be revealed by warming the walls with a hair dryer.

"Can you promise me something?" she asked, her voice disembodied in the darkness around us.

"Sure, Xal, I got nothing else to do anyway. What's up?"

"When I'm gone, read what I've written, okay?"

"I told you before, you'll be right here in the morning," I said.

"Just promise me, you have to." Her voice sounded

strained and frantic.

"Yeah, yeah, alright. You got it. I promise," I said. I heard her exhale and then I nudged over and kissed the top of her head. She shrank away but gave my hand a squeeze before rolling over.

"Goodnight, Xal."

"Goodbye, Paul."

As promised, I awoke alone the next morning. A small impression remained in the bed where Xalbadora had lain and strands of her dark hair lingered on the pillow. I rose slowly, unconcerned as to her whereabouts as I figured her to be in the shower or out walking the grounds. I noticed her glasses on a small end table that also held a diary. Rolling upright, I opened the journal to skim through the secrets of another. I smiled. Every page was blank. The paper was unmarked but not unused. The tiny book looked worn and the pages revealed creases and the residue left behind from oily fingers. I pictured her as she fidgeted compulsively with the diary. I smiled again, a bit brighter, as I gazed upon the walls and the mysteries they held.

I wove into my day slowly. I took my coffee outside and thought of Bernard. My mind became tangled in the pleasant recollection of his fantastic yarns. I got my daily helping of trivia from Randy and made a fool of myself as I tried haplessly to fend off the assault brought about from his bishops and rooks. It wasn't until midday that I got to wondering about where it was that Xal had scampered off to.

I began to ask around but no one had seen her that morning. My alarm heightened and I started to get a bit more insistent that finding Xal be made a priority. Numb to nutters and their eccentricities, the staff didn't share my concerns. It was agreed upon that the enigma that was Xalbadora would turn up soon enough. She was wont to wander off, but she always returned just as quietly as she had slipped away. I was still the new fish. It was advised that I cool my worries until I had familiarized myself a bit more with the ways of our murky little pond.

That was fair enough. The others knew her habits better than I. After all, I was fully aware that I didn't know the first thing about Xal as it were. I spent my afternoon in a charade. I played detective with a hair dryer as my only tool. I have no doubt that the noise coming from that old Conair 1200 became a bit bothersome, but I was left alone to go to it. Her message proved difficult to uncover. The print was beautiful but small. Most of the words rose to the surface in a blur while, at times, entire sentences were lost in a congealed smudge.

I switched off the hair dryer at the coming of the evening. The noise from the machine died off and was absorbed by the underlying silence. As I had spent so much time with my ears subjected to whir and hum, the quiet that greeted me felt eerie. I eased down onto the bed and looked about the room. I felt so close to Xalbadora in that moment. I had a sense of being enveloped, not by the walls around me, but by her mind. I found myself within her most private thoughts. I felt privileged and utterly confused.

Her scribblings were in Spanish, a language of which I knew not a word. This barrier aside, I couldn't make out if her message was set into blocks or columns, or if it was one unbroken stream that spiraled around one wall and onto the next. I wondered, then, if she ever meant for me to unlock her secrets. She knew me well enough to know that I was an uneducated man. For just a moment, I expected to see her emerge from the shadows to giggle at the bemusement that twisted my expression. But that was just a passing fantasy. Xalbadora kept her promises. She came over me like a refreshing breeze and left with the grace of a ghost. She wasn't coming back.

In the days and weeks that followed her vanishing, the staff and residents alike tried to uncover what it was that she had left behind. The local police got involved and took pictures of the walls, but there was only so much that they could do. Xal was an adult. She was free to leave. She wasn't with us anymore, but it took some time before she was considered missing. By then, well, the world had kept on spinning. There were other matters at hand, and with both Xalbadora and her roommate gone, there was an open room at the house. Her cryptic message got painted over, her glasses were slipped into the lost-and-found box, and a new body occupied her bed.

I never did learn what Xalbadora had wanted me to know, if there ever was anything worth knowin' in the first place. Maybe it was just gibberish born from the boredom of a mixed-up mind. I'll never know, and I'll never know what became of her. In a way, both mysteries serve to comfort me. My ignorance of such things allows me to imagine that her words were the most poetic ever penned. I can picture Xal happy, well adjusted, and successful. People go away sometimes, that's just how it goes. And of those that never come back? I like to think it's because maybe they've found someplace better to be. As for me? I didn't go anywhere, not right away, but something better was about to find me.

7. The Spaceman And The Star

There were a few others that filled out our home for wayward souls and common nutters. Most everyone else was a bit nondescript, forgettable, even, but they were of the decent sort. However, the next person that I would bond with proved different than the rest. She offered me more than fleeting and fragile companionship. She would give to me the stability and permanence I longed for but couldn't find with the likes of Randy or Bernard. She gave me something brand new, something I had never before experienced. She would give me love. Her name was Riley.

A few weeks clicked on by and life was growing stale. I missed my friends and didn't connect with the new arrivals. Restlessness wormed into me and I began to feel rather useless. My fortunes took a sunny turn once I got myself a job. Ironically enough, I secured employment at the same warehouse that had welcomed me to Nebraska earlier in the season.

I was conscious and upright for this visit, which probably aided my success at being placed on the payroll. Still, I think I was hired out of a sense of pity. That was fine by me. My new place of work was close to the halfway house and it gave me a sense of purpose. My employer specialized in flooring: laminate, carpet, tile, and so forth. My shift was overnight and my time was taken up with the tasks of stocking inventory, building displays, and readying shipments for the next morning. The work was straightforward but I enjoyed myself. During the graveyard hours, there was only a few other guys there. We played the radio loudly and goofed around on the forklifts when our chores were light.

There was a little more to it than all that, but why dwell on the details? Most everyone has a job, so there ain't much point going into the necessary things that we upright mammals do to keep roofs over our heads and food in our bellies. Change was a-happing, though. I was beginning to stow a few paychecks away, and it was a good thing, as my residency at the house was drawing to a close. I even started to feel guilty about staying there. I was taking up valuable space that could be used to comfort another, more deserving, soul. Fortunately for me, I stuck around long enough to meet the love of my life.

As the summer began to turn and die off, I took it upon myself to upkeep the grounds. This took some pressure off the staff and freed up the volunteers to put their energy into more productive matters. During my days of cuttin' grass and weeding along the property line, I noticed a new face coming 'round to visit. On a semi-regular basis, a woman would stop in to spend some time with the residents. She mainly used her time there to help out the youngest of my housemates. She gave rides to those who couldn't drive themselves and acted as something of a mentor for the youngsters who were having trouble staying right. When she saw me out in the yard, she would smile. This wasn't just a kind gesture or generic greeting. There was a true warmth in her expression. It made me feel good to see her, but I never thought much more about it. That all changed one hot evening near the start of September.

I was sitting on the steps of the porch out back. Having chewed away the afternoon working under the sun, I was drained. I closed my eyes and leaned my head back against the railing, eagerly awaiting the cool that the coming of evening would bring. I listened to the birds and the indistinct chatter as it floated out from the house. I was nearly asleep when, at once, I heard soft footsteps and the creaking of the old deck boards behind me.

"Hi, I thought maybe you could use this." The woman I had been seeing lately placed a glass of iced tea beside me. She plunked down on the opposite side of the steps and introduced herself as Riley.

"Thanks," I said. "My name's Paul."

"Are you a volunteer, too?" she asked.

"No, resident. Not for much longer, though. I'm working on getting a place of my own. I've just been trying to make myself useful around here until then."

"Oh, sorry. I wasn't trying to pry, I just figured you were maintenance or something. People tend to gossip in these places and no one has much to say about you," she said quietly.

"I ain't surprised. I guess I'm just not that interesting, since my response to pretty much every question I'm asked is nothing more than a shrug of my shoulders. I got no real answers." I could tell that Riley was trying to mask her curiosity, but I noticed her eyes as they studied me.

"Wait, are you that guy who…"

"That's me. And that's about as much as I know, unless you wanna hear about the different styles of wigs that you can buy for your dog in Japan."

"Randy?" she asked.

"Who else?" I replied, and we both laughed.

Sitting there with Riley, being in her company, hearing her laugh, it made me feel as though a bottle of pop had been shook up and turned loose under every inch of my skin. Most feelings were new to me, but this felt different. Somehow, I knew that this experience was of the type that I had always been made to go without. It made me nervous and unsure, but despite all my anxieties, it made me yearn for more.

I tried not to stare, but next to her, I found myself somewhat hypnotized. I was like a creature of the dirt that had finally clawed its way to the surface to gaze upon the sun for the first time. She seemed comfortable, naturally affectionate, and her voice hinted at the quirks of her personality. I kinda looked upon her the way a child might study a cartoon. It was as though Riley had been drawn, every aspect of her seemed to fit perfectly with the person underneath, even down to her choice of dress. A pair of little brown work boots were slid up over her jeans and she wore a red checkered tank top. A bundle of chestnut curls cascaded down her tanned shoulders, and her locks glistened red under the rays of evening. Her face was mildly sun-beaten and a field of freckles rolled out over her nose and across her cheeks. Behind her glasses, her eyes offered promises of patience and warmth.

"Have dinner with me," I said, and then immediately regretted being so blunt.

A reflexive giggle left her lips. She wasn't facing me, but her gaze came to meet mine as she fixed me with a side-eyed stare. She was trying to sort out if I was being sincere, and, in doing so, she looked suspicious and cute.

"Or," I continued, "You can just walk me inside and tell me that we went on a date. I have no idea if I've ever been on a date before, so I got no frame of reference. Oh, and if you do say yes, it won't be nothing fancy anyway. I don't make much money, and what I do make, I'm trying to save. I don't mean to sound cheap, although I might be, so maybe you could tag along while I figure that out. I get it, a guy living in a halfway house isn't much of a catch, but if nothing else, I'm something of a mystery. Girls like mysterious guys, right? I guess I have that going for me."

"Yeah, girls like mystery. Well, I don't know about all of us, but I do, or I did. I dated a mysterious guy once. Then we had a kid, got married, and had another kid. A little trashy, a little traditional. Don't judge, dude. Then, once he stopped being mysterious, he started being a dick," she explained, comically. "He was banging some chick from work and about every other girl in the state that would sleep with him. We got divorced due to the extra-marital humping, you know. He pays child support whenever he damn well pleases and acts like I should think he's the father of the year for making time to see his own kids once a month. I work fulltime, volunteer here when the asshat has the kids, and I'm probably a decade older than you. Long story short, this chick comes with baggage," she said with mock pride as she pointed both of her thumbs back at herself. "So, I'm willing to roll the dice on mystery and dinner, as long as you know what you're getting into. You might want to make a mental note that I'm partial to fried chicken. Your move, spaceman."

"Spaceman?" I asked.

"Well, you fell outta the sky, right?"

"Technically, yeah. Although I imagine that you're exaggerating my fall just a bit."

"Particulars, dude. Whatever. So, are you stalling or am I getting fried chicken in the near future?" she challenged.

"Umm, it looks like I'm buying you dinner," I said.

8. Coming Together

Fall arrived and with it came a myriad of changes. Picking up overtime at the warehouse allowed me to wave goodbye to my friends at the halfway house. I rented a small apartment in town. The second story window at the front of my place overlooked a small park. There were playground amusements set up for children to play on, and a small gazebo sat near the center of the park. Its function was nothing higher than to add additional charm to an already pleasant environment. An old school house down the street had been turned into a post office.

A diner, that seemed to be the oldest business in Stone Horse, functioned like a church. It was a place for the residents of the community to start or end their days and to catch up with friends. I was immediately comfortable there. I've heard the Midwest tagged with the unflattering moniker *the flyover states.* If that was how others viewed Nebraska, so be it. I was happy to be somewhere that the rest of the country mostly ignored. Let the world pass us on by. Back then, a quiet life spent with Riley was the paradise I always needed but was too dumb to seek out. I wouldn't have traded it for anything. It's just too bad that the gamble wasn't always up to me.

I continued to date Riley and, had the choice been mine, I would have loved to move in to her place, kids and all. But when it came time for me to leave the halfway house and track down somewhere else to live, she didn't offer and I wasn't gonna ask. Though we carried on like two halves of a complete being, always meant to be joined, she tried her best to scare me off in the early goings. She steered our conversations into the complicated realms of parenthood and failed marriage. If she reminded me once that she was thirty-three years old, she did so thirty-three times. She made sure that I was aware of the close bond she had with her younger sister. She was also rather emphatic in her explanation of how kid sister, Julia, was a bit of a hot-head with the protective instincts of a pit bull. I didn't blink. None of that gave me cause for hesitation. I was sharp enough to understand that she was testing my sincerity. If she would have me, I planned on sticking around.

A layer of discarded leaves danced over the street and a chilly rain clawed at the windows of the diner. Riley and me were inside, picking at the few remaining fries left scattered on our plates. Her ex had the kids for the weekend and she had just come from my old place of residence. Even though I had taken a bite out of her time, she never neglected the needs of those less fortunate. The responsibility she felt to those people was self-imposed, but that just made her all the more vigilant. To this day, I can't figure how nature stuffed a heart that big into a body so small.

"Riles, I love you." We hadn't been dating long, and I knew I was taking a risk, but I didn't care. I loved her, and when someone that special is loved, they deserve to know.

"Dude!" she said in a sweet but exasperated voice. She leaned back in the booth and folded her arms across her chest.

"You don't have to say nothing."

"Yeah, I kinda do, that's the thing," she replied quietly.

"Honestly, I'm cool. I mean, if you want to say something, okay, but we can talk about whatever," I said.

"Ugh, now you're just trying to be cute."

"Is it working?" I asked sheepishly.

"Yeah, it usually does. Anyway, there's something that we need to get out of the way first. Just how old are you?"

"I don't know, you know that," I said.

"Perfect! I feel a little pervy knowing that when I graduated high school, you were probably still collecting Power Rangers dolls. So, how do you feel about being 29, maybe even 30?" she asked.

"Okay, not cool. They're called action figures, not dolls, and I have no idea if I collected them or not. But, if I did, I definitely called them action figures. As for the age thing? 30, sure, whatever. 29 or 99, I don't care as long as it makes you happy."

"Rad," she said slowly, widening her eyes for comedic effect. "Hey, Paul?"

"Yeah?" I asked.

"I love you, too."

From that moment, I would like to be able to say that our relationship unfolded in the pleasant and magical ways of fictitious love as it is woven in the movies. Things went on good, but it was work. There was a methodical and plodding pace to the evolution of our union. All that's natural, I suppose, what with the complications of children, the baggage of previous failures, and the everyday tasks the come laced into an ordinary life. The truth was, I wanted Riley all to myself.

This wasn't a malicious jealousy, it was just the raw feelings of the boy I never got to be and no longer remembered. But, mostly, these were just thoughts that tugged at me during the nights I spent alone in my apartment, longing for the day when we would spend all of our nights together.

The season crept on and the chill of winter seeped into every shortened day. I took to spending more time hanging around Riley's kids. Her daughter, Hannah, was ten years old and had inherited her mom's sarcasm. Riley was always trying to correct Hannah's manners as she went about asking me whatever happened to pop into her head or busting my chops over the shortcomings of my damaged brain. I never took no offense to her questions. I often found her nature endearing, and laughed any time she said something that her mom deemed inappropriate. Riley would put on a good show of admonishing me for encouraging bad behavior, but she couldn't hide the sparkle in her eye as she watched her daughter take a shine to me.

Her son, Charlie, he was twelve and a whole different puzzle. The boy was of the quieter sort. He was polite to me but still viewed my presence at his mom's side as that of an imposter. I couldn't rightly fault him. His dad had been displaced by divorce and was then in the process of being replaced in the family. In some ways, I think he was suspicious of me. Perhaps some of Aunt Julia's skepticism had found his ear. That was fair enough. I was willing to prove myself worthy.

During those early days of winter, I tried my best to play handyman around Riley's place. I'm pretty sure she knew more about electrical outlets and plumbing than I did, but I did what I could, and my clumsy efforts freed her up to be mom for a few extra minutes here and there. It made me feel good to be able to contribute, not just to us as a couple, but to us as a family. It helped me to bond with Hannah as well. She liked to pal around and hand me tools. She'd giggle delightedly any time I swore while striking an errant blow with a hammer or if I zipped myself on a live wire. Charlie still remained unimpressed, but I did catch a smile wiggle into the corner of his mouth as I helped him to string an old guitar that he'd gotten as a birthday present.

On the nights that I spent playing house over at Riley's, we'd usually end our time together with a walk. Riley's house sat along a rural stretch of forgotten road that butted up against an old cornfield. The abandoned crop came up in patches, with weeds and other plant life growing wild and unchecked. Her and I would walk, flanked by the vegetation, and do nothing more than enjoy the company of one another. It was our time to be alone, as the kids would usually entertain themselves far from the boring activities of dull adults. I liked these moments, but they all came with a bittersweet taste, for I knew that the time for me to return to the quiet of my apartment was drawing near.

As we walked in silence, I watched as the withered husks brushed Riley's shoulders. They touched her gently, intentionally, it seemed, as though she were as important to them as water and light. I held her hand in mine and admired the last rays of daylight as they danced among her hair as it cascaded down from a knit cap. Surrounded by the splendor that nature can bring, we kissed and then she laid her head on my chest.

"You wanna spend the night, dude?" she asked, quietly.

"That's probably not going to go over too well with Charlie," I said.

"Aww, I know," she said, rubbing her forehead. "I still think of him as a little boy, but he's growing up. The thing is, to him, you're still just some guy that's doing his mom. He's a little bent over it, you know?"

"It's okay, Riles. I get it. This is the only place I wanna be, but we don't have to force nothing," I said.

"That's just it, dude. We're not forcing anything. Everything about this is right. You're great with the kids. Hannah adores you. Charlie will come around. He'll see what I see, that you're not just some guy who's doing his mom. You are so much more than that. It kills me to send you away all the time. I don't want you on a part-time basis. You belong here."

It felt like I'd waited a lifetime to hear those words. Hearing her give voice to what I had always hoped was true built something up inside me. It made me feel as though all the scattered aspects of who I was were coming together to form a complete person. I always kinda knew that I didn't *need* my old memories, but, in that moment, I knew I no longer even wanted them. All that mattered was what happened from that point forward.

"I love you," I said. "and, you know, since I'm sleeping over tonight, we don't have to go right to sleep."

"Let's baby-step this thing, Spaceman. Charlie does sleep right across the hall. I'd feel pretty bad if he cracked that guitar over your head mid-shag," she said with a smile.

"Yeah, good point. Let's go home."

9. Home

As it turned out, I had to temper my enthusiasm and curb my joy as the meaning of *home* still came hollow to my ears. I had an apartment lease that I couldn't afford to break, and Riley's former husband, Blaine, weren't too keen on me sharing a roof with his kids. He made a fuss and was generally difficult until Riley caved. With her kids in mind, she did what was necessary to maintain civility with their father. I knew it was the right move, but it hurt nonetheless. I wanted to resent Blaine for it, but, truth be told, he was alright. He had done wrong by Riley and, in turn, he had let his children down. The thing is, he felt that, and spoke to me regretfully over the distance he had put between himself and his family. Like all men, he wasn't perfect. He did seem to bring happiness to Charlie and Hannah, though, even if he wasn't around as much as he should have been.

And so it went. I stayed in town over the winter. I found

myself alone much of the time. Harsh weather conspired to keep me from Riley for many a night. I didn't have much frame of reference for weather of any sort, but I soon realized that the turn of one year to the next came red of tooth and claw to the Midwest. I spent time doing much of nothing besides watching the slow tick of the clock and petitioning the calendar to get on with the business of spring.

When February rolled around, I got mired in something of a depression. The holidays had come and gone and, though enjoyable, those occasions served to remind me that I was still indeed an outsider to common existence. If not for the charity of my girlfriend and the tolerance of her family, I had nothing. I began to feel that I was leaning a bit too hard on my relationship with Riley. I knew that I was taking more than I could possibly return. It was during these grayest moments of a deadening Midwest winter that I set about bettering myself for the life I hoped to have.

I picked up all the overtime that was on offer. I got myself a more reliable car and worked weekends at the local hardware store. I took to the task of familiarizing myself with the broader aspects of what it took to be a passable handyman. I helped out repairing snow blowers and small engine equipment, figuring that such skills might serve me well in my rural environment. The girl who worked the cash register at Custer's hardware was pretty slick with a guitar, or, at least, I thought so. She was kind enough to teach me some chords and guide me through the workings of simple songs. I didn't recognize most of the songs she taught me and, sure enough, they probably would do little to impress Charlie, but I was gonna try all the same. I hadn't made much progress with him over the winter. I was hoping that with music in common, maybe we could finally have a go at bonding.

During the early days of March, I was getting a haircut and thinking impatiently of the mild season to come. I had practical transportation, some newly acquired, albeit shaky, skills, and with little time left on my apartment lease, I was financially balanced enough to break the contract. I was feelin' fresh and feelin' good. And that's when Julia paid me a visit.

I was walking back home, enjoying the pleasant temperature and the sunlight, when I spied Julia coming from the opposite direction. She was heading for my apartment, but upon sighting me, she put her boots to purpose as she turned her walk into a march. As I watched her advance, I took to thinking about how closely she resembled Riley, only rendered in a funhouse mirror. With these subtle changes, Julia was even prettier than her sister, or could have been. But there was something that was just off kilter. It was the kindness, the cuteness, that wasn't there. The younger Ms. Taylor had insulated herself with jagged edges and rough surfaces. I bristled and found myself somewhat frightened. It was weird for me, experiencing something of a fear over a small young woman who had never shown me aggression. Sure, Julia had an inexhaustible supply of prickly quips and dagger-eyed glances to shoot my way, but she was not unkind to me. Still, something deep within me remained unsettled. It got me to thinking about the trauma that had placed me in Nebraska nearly a year before. Maybe something buried in the black of my mind was reacting, trying frantically to kick its way to the surface. It might have all been nonsense, but before I had any more think time to dedicate to the grip of unusual feelings, Julia came upon me.

"Grab some bench, dude," instructed Julia sternly, as she pointed to the park across the street.

"What's up, Jules?" I asked, although I already had sussed out what was on her mind.

"Save the cute nicknames for Riley," she said as she brushed away a coating of snow from the bench, sat down, and lit a cigarette.

"My bad," I said, as I sat down beside her.

"Are you?" she asked.

"What now?"

"Bad," she said, with some measure of authority. "No one

knows shit about you. And I want to know if you're bad. See, my gullible goof of a sister has a thing for ending up with bad dudes. The breakup with Blaine really fucked with her for a while. I gotta know that you're not gonna do the same."

"Listen, Jules, Julia," I quickly corrected myself as I noticed her eyes narrow into slits. "Even *I* don't know what I was like before, but, you know me, right? I'm not a bad guy, am I? I love Riley. I want to be with her. And I want you to be okay with that. It's important to me." I said.

"Why?" she asked, testing me.

"Because you're her family. Riley adores you, and not just 'cause she has to. She thinks the world of you. I mean, I kinda think you're a pain in the ass, but whatever."

"I told you before, don't try and be cute," she said, as she took to clicking her Zippo lighter open and shut again. I began to wonder if she had notions of setting me on fire. "Look, you know what bothers me?" she went on. "Is that one day you're gonna remember who you are, and we're going to find out that you're already married, or a mob boss, or a terrorist, or something."

I laughed, but it didn't feel good. "I don't know if that'll ever happen but, if it does, it won't change nothing. I love your sister, end of story. Hey, I was probably just some ordinary loser before this, anyway."

"Yeah, you're probably right about that," she said, with just a little poison on her tongue.

"So, you gonna be there to help me move in?" I asked.

"Oh, yeah, I'll be there, Spaceman," she said, using Riley's favorite nickname for me in as menacing a tone as possible. "And if you hurt her, I will beat your ass straight back to the moon."

"Sounds good. See you for the big day, Jules," I said, unable to resist the urge to needle her a bit.

"See ya later, fuckface," Julia said dryly as she got up from the bench and started away.

The day that I moved in with Riley sticks with me like the

events of that day were rubbed in adhesive, flung against my mind, and sewn in place. That assessment don't sound real good and that's because it ain't. It's a beautiful memory, but it's the one that haunts me above all others. For just a while, time stopped. Everything was perfect. If only things could have remained that way.

Anyway, on that fateful day, the weather was warm and the clouds parted to reveal an all-enveloping blue sky dotted by a bright orange sun. As the process of the move wound on, I seemed to watch the particulars of the day unfold from outside myself, like I was caught in a dream. It all felt surreal, the kids shuttling the lighter boxes inside, Riley's cousins shifting things around in the garage and living room, all the while suffering orders from Julia. I recall as Julia made sure that I noticed the suspicion in her eyes, but I was also able to uncover the playfulness that hid behind the pierce of her stare. And I'll never forget the way Riley looked. Her hair pulled back and tucked under a ballcap, her sleeves rolled up, and the mud along the bottoms of her jeans as the mild weather melted away the snow and turned her driveway into a marsh. But most of all, I remember her face. The way she smiled, the happiness in her eyes, was truly unforgettable.

And that's how it all began, my twenty years of peace and joy. I settled in that night and never felt out of place. At long last, there was somewhere I belonged. That first year we spent under one roof sped on past with not much of note taking place. I think that was the best part. Me, Riley, the kids, all of us as one, we just came together and found happiness as a family. Our jobs, responsibilities, and obligations remained the same, but every task seemed easier.

Hannah continued to follow me around like a puppy and gave to me the moniker of dad 2.0. After many a nice night spent out back fiddling around on our guitars, Charlie decided that I wasn't so bad after all. Even Julia warmed up to me. She never stopped giving me a hard time, but that was just pride getting in the way of sweetness. Or, maybe, that was her way of finally being sweet to me. Hell, even Blaine took a liking to me. Riley talked about him like he was a true bastard, but he was okay. I imagine, for her, the shadows of their divorce had darkened his image in her eyes. Blaine saw I wasn't trying to replace him as a father and he realized that I made Riley happy. I admire the man for the respect he showed towards me. Riles found me buddying up to her ex a bit strange at first, but she came to appreciate the efforts made by the both of us. This served to bring her and I closer and it mended some of the wounds shared by her and the father of her children.

"We've been together over a year now," Riley whispered to me one night as we lay in bed.

"I know. It's been the best year of my life."

"Yeah, dude, but I just thought of something," she said, sitting up. "You've probably had a birthday somewhere in there. I can't believe we never talked about that. God, I'm sorry. I feel like such a spaz."

"You know, I could probably parlay this guilt trip you're having into something sweet but, if I'm being honest, I ain't thought of it either," I said.

"You wanna pick a date?" she asked.

"Sure. Umm, how about March 27th?" I said.

"Was that the day we moved in together?"

"Yeah. I can't think of a better date. It's when my life began, Riles."

"March 27th it is," she said, kissed me softly, and rolled over.

"You still feeling guilty?" I asked, poking her in the ribs.

"Dude, I got to work in like five hours. Call a hooker or something," she said with a yawn.

"I wonder if your sister's still up," I said sheepishly into the air, to which Riley laughed almost uncontrollably.

"Oh, man, please try and hit on Julia. I would pay good money to see that. But then I'd have to pay for your funeral *and* get a new boyfriend. I'm getting too old to play the field. Stay alive and go to bed," she said, reaching over to pat my leg.

"I love you, baby," I said, and closed my eyes.

10. Echoes

The years wound on and all the charms of common domesticity settled down over our house. As the kids grew, their days were filled with activities and new interests. With a heavy heart, Riley stopped doing consistent volunteer work. She took a job working the office for a local farm equipment dealer. The hours were good and the pay was better than expected. She still made an effort to pop in around my old halfway house and other such places around town. This gave her a chance to catch up with some of the friends she had made over the years, but there simply wasn't time for much else. Even with me around to pick up some slack, the pace of life seemed to accelerate. I stayed on at the warehouse and received a promotion. It wasn't nothing fancy, but between Riles and myself, we began earning a comfortable income. It was time that always seemed in short supply.

The kids had grown into teenagers and, as such, every day became a whirlwind of activity. Hannah took to sports. I think she held a position on every team in her high school. It appeared there wasn't an athletic endeavor too challenging for that girl to master. She even went through a phase of wanting to race stock cars. I had to break the news to her that we weren't of the means to fund such an activity. She took the letdown well, though. In lieu of commanding an 800 horsepower dream machine, she settled on running my truck through the dirt trails behind the house. Now, it wasn't that nice to begin with, but that truck was never clean again.

I didn't pay such details any mind. I could do nothing but smile. Before I gave that old Dodge over to the mud of the boneyard, it served as another way for daughter and dad 2.0 to bond. We spent many a night out in the garage trying our best to replace clutches, leaf springs, and whatever others parts Hannah saw fit to torture that week. I still had no idea about who I was before Nebraska, but as Hannah outshined me concerning all things automotive, I knew for damned sure that I was no mechanic.

Charlie was just weeks away from graduation. Helping him to such a point proved to be a hell of a task. That boy was sharp as a blade, but the ways of structured schooling didn't suit him. Like his sister, Charlie outpaced me in our common interests. He produced sounds from the guitar that I couldn't even dream of replicating. He had entertained the notion of applying to the Berklee College of Music, but didn't see it through. What that young man really loved was to paint. He may have been an even better artist than a musician.

At times we butted heads, especially when he was in his early teens. On more than one occasion he pulled the *you're not my real dad* line when what I asked of him was deemed unfair. If I really put thought to it though, I think our disagreements came more from the nature of a growing man than anything else. He had to test me. All this was expected, and I got it.

I know he always valued the support I showed to him, no matter the nature of his interests. This was what stuck us together. However impractical or financially suspect his goals seemed, he knew I'd be there in his corner. In return, he kept the teenager's favored pastime of being difficult to a minimum. It was a fair trade. He was a good kid. He's a better man. I couldn't have asked for more and I wouldn't have it any other way.

There were a few bumps in the road during these times. They were happy days, no doubt, but change often comes with a touch of the sour. Just after Charlie bid adieu to high school, Blaine and his new wife packed up and headed south. He had remarried a year or so before and took on a set of stepkids. Not long after the wedding, he and the wife added a new addition to the family. He was a good father, but practical to a fault, and it was Charlie and Hannah that bore the brunt of his flaws.

Hannah and her brother felt that Blaine had less time for them. They felt replaced. I can't argue with their assessment. To their father, though, he saw them as young adults. They were no longer children, and so Blaine took something of a hands-off approach with them moving forward. I didn't like it, how this distance seemed to wound the kids. But when I get down to the bare facts of it all, there are only so many hours in the day. He had taken on the responsibility of setting another man's offspring on the right path. I could sympathize with the complications. Blaine also had a new baby to raise. I think this is why he opted to move away. Somewhere in his mind, he knew that if he stayed he couldn't properly care for any of his children. So, he chose and the original, older models lost out.

Down in Texas, he took a job working for a drilling outfit. From what I heard, the pay was impressive. We parted amicably. I even helped him pack up the house, but that was where things ended between me and him. He flew up a couple of times a year to see the kids but always maintained a distance with Riley and myself. He had moved on and there was nothing beyond Charlie and Hannah that remained to tether Blaine to Nebraska. I think he liked it that way.

To the surprise of no one, Julia couldn't be rid of him fast enough, but much to my surprise, the distance took to bothering Riley. I came to understand it. Her children were a constant reminder of the man she once saw herself dying beside, deep into the reaches of old age. I imagine that the reality of Blaine becoming little more than a stranger to her bit at Riley more than she had expected, if she expected it at all.

It took my Riley the better part of a year to surface from the funk of Blaine's departure. Just as she was coming out of it, another, more significant, event rolled over the horizon of our lives. Riley's parents pulled up stakes and left the only home they had ever known for a new life in New Mexico. In their sixties, financially comfortable and retired, the option to leave behind Midwest winters for good was an obvious choice. They were affable people, and relatively healthy. They didn't fancy winding out their lives staring into endless fields of corn from a back porch devoid of activity. They wanted adventure and new challenges. It was their time.

I suppose no matter how well thought out or intentioned such a thing can be, it's still a difficult process for a child to endure. Riley was a thirty-nine-year-old woman, but when she calculated all those hundreds of miles put between her and her parents, she became a child again. And, like a child, she once more viewed her parents not as individuals with their own desires, but as her personal well of comfort. She became selfish, resentful, even, but mostly she was just sad. Her parents promised to visit often and they were ever true to their word. To Riley, though, they might as well have shipped off to the red plains of Mars.

Blaine, the father of her children, had been gone awhile by this point and, with every passing year, he became less real and more memory of the failures of the past. And that's when reality really struck Riley; her kids would be the next to go. I felt her sadness and I shared in it. There was more to it for me than all that, however. I knew that she would need me to step up. In a fashion, I felt I had graduated. In the years that followed, it was up to me to truly prove myself worthy of her companionship and love.

I was feelin' good and hopeful for the future. A little time had passed and Riley took to processing the events of late with a clearer mind. She came around to understand the choices made by others, and, in a moment that touched my heart, she admitted to me that I was the father-figure she wanted for the kids. I teared up when she told me that I was the father that they deserved. It was her omission of the word *figure* that nearly broke me. I was sniffling like a baby and took on the full force of a wave of Riley's sarcasm as she went about razzing me over my sensitivity. For the first time in months, I witnessed her sense of humor return. I knew we were gonna be alright.

I like a good joke, and I loved the way she poked fun at me. Hell, it was only when she wasn't giving me a hard time that I grew concerned. But there was one remark she made that stirred something dark within me. It was just a passing comment. It was meant to be funny, and it was, but there was just something about what she said that upturned a bit of the earth that lay over my memories. It came, as such things often do, unexpectedly. We were out having dinner with my old adversary, Julia. The three of us were putting back beers and munching through platters of chicken wings. I wasn't sayin' much. Riles and Julia were having a good time chatting amongst themselves and I was content to sit there and listen. Eventually, though, base needs caused me to chime in and interrupt the sister talk.

"Hey, Jules, you gonna finish those?" I asked, motioning toward the remaining hot wings that had sat neglected on her plate for the last twenty minutes.

"You know," she began, bringing one of the wings up to her lips. "You would think that after all these years, you'd know better than to call me Jules and then ask for something."

"So, that's a no?" I asked, sarcastically.

"Umm, these are so good," she said, slowly. Just to taunt me, Julia closed her eyes in mock pleasure as she skinned a drumstick with her teeth.

"I seem to remember you bitchin' about them being too hot," I said.

"It'll be worth it," she replied with a huff, sweat breaking on her forehead.

"You guys are idiots," said Riley. I just shrugged my shoulders and went about dipping celery sticks in bleu cheese.

"Ha! That's right, asshat. Enjoy your celery while I eat all these delicious wings." Julia was practically crying at this point, but she wasn't gonna give it up until her plate held nothing but a pile of bones. Needling me was just too much fun for her.

"I hope you get throw-up in your hair later," I joked, dryly.

"Is this why we never married?" Riley asked of me.

"What now, babe? I don't think hot wings ever factored into that decision," I said.

"No, I'm wondering if we never got married because you guys already did. The two of you bicker like an old married couple."

"Oh, forget that noise, sis. I'd go full lez before I'd bang this loser," said Julia as she pointed at me with a finger wet with sauce.

"Okay, now I'm actually offended," I said. "What's so wrong with me? You've banged everyone else."

Riley kicked me under the table, but she couldn't stop herself from laughing either. The look on Julia's face suggested that she desperately wanted to continue hurling barbs in my direction, but the scorch of habanero robbed her of voice. In that moment, the highest insult she could manage was to swipe my beer. In short order, she downed the drink and then dabbed her eyes with a napkin. Her lips bent into a witch's grin as she shot me the finger.

We sat around for a while longer and got another couple rounds of drinks. Me and Julia continued to jab at one another. We had gone on like this since the start, but during the past year or so, this way of carrying on became our way to bond. It was how we went about showing one another affection. She gave everybody crap. Maybe that's why she had trouble keeping a man in her life. I think she actually took to favoring my company once I had proved that I could handle the jagged aspects of her attitude and serve it all back at her. I was having fun, maybe a little too much fun, trading vulgarities with my unofficial sister-in-law. Sometime during my verbal joust with Julia, I noticed that Riley had grown quiet. I looked over and saw the distance in her eyes.

"Riles, you alright?" I asked.

"Oh shit, dude. I know that look," said Julia. "Too many beers, man."

"Ugh, she's right," said Riley, running her hands through her hair. "It's the same shit every time. I have a few beers and feel awesome. I have a few more and, bam! I turn into an emotional fucking mess. I'm fine, baby. I'm fine," she assured me with a dismissive wave of her hand, as a few tears streaked down her face.

"What's going on?" asked Julia, elbowing her sister in the ribs.

"I was just thinking about the kids," Riley whispered.

"Oh, Christ. See, this is reason number 9,708 why I never had any. They just fuck around with your life, you know? I mean, don't get me wrong, I love being able to play the spastic aunt but, shit, kids are like emotional machine guns. They'll shoot you full of holes, honey."

I shot a sharp glance over to Julia and made a lowering motion with my hands. I was hoping she would tone it down just a bit as Riley wasn't in the right frame of mind to hear jokes about the challenges of child-raising.

"Yeah, my bad," said Julia. "Your kids are great, sis. Whattaya got to be worried about?"

"They are great. They're fun and independent and creative. But, pretty soon, they're gonna do all that away from me," Riley said with a pout, her tears drying.

"I'll still be here," I said.

"Some consolation prize," muttered Julia under her breath.

"Julia, you are an amazing bitch," said Riley, flatly, but with love all the same. "I'm just feeling older. I'm worried that we'll end up being one of those old empty-nest couples that drinks overpriced wine at the Cheesecake Factory and wastes away our evenings watching reruns of Seinfeld or Big Bang or something, and talking about how culturally *important* those shows were. I don't want to be old and lame."

Riley went on a bit more and she no doubt peppered her lament with cute scenarios, but my mind went somewhere else. I felt my concentration break down. My vision went fuzzy. My focus, in all respects, went away, like the tide retreating from the shore. I felt nauseous. I shuddered under the onslaught of anxiety and a cold sweat was pushed out of my pores. I watched as the water dropped from off my face. My shirt was soaked and my skin felt clammy. I took to shivers. The room spun and it darkened. This wasn't a blacking-out of my surroundings. Rather, it was like something lay obscured behind a wall of smoke. I had no notion of what that could be, but I felt a great sensation of dread. A creature, terrible and full of diseases, had come to visit. It wanted to tell me stories.

"Baby, you feeling okay?" I heard Riley's voice as though it had been filtered through muddy water and sediment. My ears picked up her query, but nothing registered.

"Yo, Paul, dude, you with us?" asked Julia as she snapped her fingers in front of my face. "Hey, what the fuck, you alright?"

When the relatively calm sounds of her fingers failed to retrieve me from where I had gone, Julia clapped her hands together. The sudden and sharp noise hit me like the bang of thunder. I was honestly startled. It was only for a moment, but I recoiled into a defensive position. In my eyes, there laid fear, authentic and naked. Riley saw it. Julia saw it. They both fell into silence and studied me like a mysterious museum exhibit.

"I just don't feel very well," I said weakly. "Can we go now, please?"

Riley helped me to my feet and we made for home. Julia elected to stay behind at the bar. She covered her concerns as she voiced desires for more alcohol and a prospect of nabbing a short-term boyfriend. In my wobbly state, I saw right through the lies. Julia was scared and suspicious. She may have accepted me into the family but, in the back of her mind, in the corners of her eyes, the doubts remained.

"Hey, Paul, be okay, okay?" she said once I had reached the exit. Julia rarely called me by name and she was loath to say anything to me that didn't come coupled to an insult. I knew then that she held genuine concern for me. It made me feel loved, and it made me feel afraid.

After we arrived home, I went up to bed and Riley spent a little time with the kids. She busied herself by tidying up the house a bit and put a Crockpot together for the next day's meal. Although it was late, Charlie was given the keys to the car. He was delighted at this gesture of freedom, a freedom that his mother curtly reminded him was a fragile privilege. Hannah groaned when her request for a night out was denied. She retreated to her room and played music just loud enough to annoy us. She was unhappy, and she made sure we were alerted to this by playing songs that she knew particularly bothered her mother and me. Ever a sharp girl, Hannah kept the volume reasonable enough to ward off parental protestations for as long as could be expected.

After what seemed an eternity, Riley joined me in the bedroom. I was atop the mattress but still dressed. Sleep had failed to find me. I was in a daze but too bothered by the unknown to surrender to unconsciousness.

"Are you feeling better?" Riley asked softly as she sat beside me and patted my leg.

"Yeah, I'm good. I just got a little shook up is all."

"Did you...did you remember something?" she asked, cautiously.

"No. But I feel like I almost did. It scared me and I don't know why. I don't even know what set this off. Who knows, maybe I choked on a chicken bone when I was five and got all worked up over it. It's nothing now. It don't matter," I said.

"Yeah it does. You were someone before us. You have a past. One day we might have to deal with that. Maybe you should talk to someone."

"I don't wanna talk to no one. I told you before, I don't care about who I was before this. I don't. It don't matter," I said.

"You really are afraid of what you might find out, aren't you? Aren't you even a little curious? I'd want to know, I think," Riley said.

"I guess I wonder about it sometimes. But I kinda wonder about my past the way I wonder about Amelia Earhart. It don't affect my life. It seems too damn distant. It don't matter, Riles, it just don't matter." I trailed off and she looked at me once I grew quiet. Her stare wasn't quite hard, but it didn't feel soft either. I exhaled shakily. I did so like a reflex. Behind this action, Riley saw that there was more hiding.

"Just get it out, dude," she pleaded, laying her hand over

mine.

"Okay, yeah, fair enough," I said with another shuddering breath. "I never have remembered anything. That's the truth. But, sometimes I feel like there's this thing that's chasing me. Every once in a while, it gets close. I try and hide from it. I try to hide it..." I did my best to explain, but my thoughts again wandered away.

"Hey, if it catches you, you ain't going to be alone," she said.

"I know, baby, I know. It's just, I feel like I'm standing on thin ice. I have this dream sometimes. I'm out on the ice. The water below is dark, and every so often I catch a glimpse of something right below the surface. I can't ever make out what it is, but I'm scared of it. Somewhere inside me, I know it ain't good. I'm terrified of it coming up through, or me falling in, I guess. I'm always on the surface, but I get the sensation that I'm drowning. And then the weirdest thing happens. I hear a laugh. Not like a menacing laugh or nothing. It's a girl's laugh. Kinda bubbly, almost, and then I wake up." I looked at Riley and, to my surprise, she was unfazed.

"Scary ice bitch, huh? Are you sure that you're not just having nightmares about my sister?" Riley said with a smile.

I couldn't have loved her more than in that moment. She knew there weren't no solution or cure for what was getting at me. All she could do for me then was to medicate my ills. She made me laugh. With a few words, she reduced my monsters to silly things of no consequence. Finally, I felt as my eyelids went heavy. I passed out in a matter of minutes and was granted the mercy of dreamless sleep.

11. Screams

As the natural course of time would have it, the kids moved out and set off to discover their own lives. Charlie got in at a liberal arts school in New York City. We all knew that there probably weren't no money to be made with such a degree, but it was what Charlie wanted to do. I wasn't gonna protest. We all got just one life, might as well make it count. As mothers tend to be, Riley was fully behind her son's decision. And, as mothers are also wont to do, Riley was worried out of her skull. Just the words *New York* gave her the shivers. The leap he took gave me anxiety and I wasn't going anywhere. Sure, I didn't know where I came from, but any town larger than Stone Horse seemed rather intimidating to me. I don't think it was the specter of crime and grime and so forth that concerned us. Our worries more or less stemmed from the scale of everything in a big city. To me and Riley, it all sounded overwhelming. But, hell, we got to stay behind with the corn and the quiet. What was more, Charlie was positively struck by lightning with excitement. That boy had a passion and he was fixing on seeing it chased down.

Right before Hannah struck out on her own, Riles and me flew up to visit Charlie. He had a year left with his studies, and had recently taken up residence just outside of Manhattan. It was so much bigger than I ever imagined. The lights, the noises, the sheer number of people put me in awe. There was so much stimuli to process that I allowed myself to get lost in the blur of it all. I happily played the part of ignorant yokel and gave the reins over to Charlie. We went where he wanted and got our dinners from street vendors. I asked him a thousand stupid questions and took just as many stupid pictures. If there ever was an obvious tourist, I was him. I moved too slow for the natives and my nerves about worked me into a puke any time me and Riley had to catch a subway without the guiding hand of our son.

To my surprise, Riley wasn't fazed a bit. She loved every last second that we spent among the utter domination of concrete, steel, and bright lights. There was a glow in her eyes the entire trip. It didn't much seem to matter what we was up to. She enjoyed every aspect of what New York City had to offer. Central park, Times Square, the utter chaos of Chinatown, didn't matter. She was like a kid that got to celebrate Christmas in the living room of Santa Claus himself. She engaged with the street performers and toyed around playfully with every colorful character that approached us. She sang karaoke with a drag queen at a gay bar and joined in with the silliness that some dance troupe put on as they overtook Battery Park for the better part of fifteen minutes.

We only stayed for three days, but by the waning hours of our first afternoon there, I was exhausted. Mother and son took to razzing me over my fatigue and general inability to keep up with the whirlwind. For the first time in our relationship, Riley delighted in reminding me that she was older than me.

What's the matter, punk, can't you keep up with this cougar? She shouted that very line to me one time when she outpaced me by half a block. She made a clawing motion with her hands and meowed at me in comedic fashion. I sighed in defeat and hurried my pace, and, as for Charlie, he was a bit embarrassed.

It was a great trip, and something that Riley and me had denied ourselves for far too long. Up until this point we never went away, just the two of us. Hell, that was the first time that we had stayed in a hotel without the kids. The room we rented was on the Upper West Side. It was barely bigger than a closet and each night was about the cost of a car payment for a new SUV. It was worth every dime.

By the time we had settled in for what would be our last night in Manhattan, I had warmed to the charms of this strange land. As Riley set about taking off her makeup, I stood out on the tiny balcony and took in my surroundings, and the sounds of a city that never shut its eyes to sleep. There was a magic to it. The way everything fit together and somehow managed to work. The way so many of the people seemed to move with purpose. I marveled at children as they navigated this labyrinth that would see a minotaur get turned around. It may not have been where I was from, and it probably wasn't where I belonged, but I found a love for the city. It wasn't so much for what it had given to me, but for what it had given to Riley. It permitted her to let loose, to be a little weird. It welcomed and rewarded her colorful personality.

"Screw the 401k, dude. I got it all figured out," Riley said to me as we laid down to sleep in that rented room.

"I'm listenin'," I muttered, sleepily.

"Remember the old chick with the feathered headdress and the accordion?" she asked.

Such a spectacle isn't exactly the type of thing that slips the mind once seen. The woman in question was a street performer, probably in her sixties. She wore Native American garb, even though she was Asian, played an accordion to entertain passersby, and propped up a sign that read *your generous donations will go to fund my base necessities of gigolos, burritos, and kittens. Cod bless.* Beside this there was a crude drawing of a fish. I have no idea why.

"No, babe, can't seem to bring her to mind," I said.

"That's my plan. By the time I'm that age, she'll be dead and there'll be a hole in the market for old crazy chicks that play accordions for googly-eyed tourists. It's perfect. Maybe Julia will want to team up. I imagine she could play the drums, since she's a spaz," said Riley.

"What about me?"

"You're tall. You'd make the perfect queen. You could be our mascot. Dance around and stuff, you know?"

"So, let me get this, you and your sister are gonna be insane street biddies, and I'm going to be flailing around in drag for the amusement of strangers?" I asked.

"Well, not just strangers. We'd dig it, too."

"Ah, why the hell not? There are plenty of retirement plans that sound pretty boring. This ain't one of them. Sure, I'm in," I said.

I felt a giggle weave its way through Riley as, I imagined, she pictured the two of us sliding into our golden years in magnificently bizarre fashion. It was just seconds later that I heard her begin to lightly snore. I love you, New York. You're almost as amazing as Riley.

There were a few speed bumps encountered along the path

of our urban adventure, however. I wish it had been all oversized pizza slices, tourist jitters, and cheap souvenirs, but that ain't the way it went down. I had a few episodes there. The meaning of such things I was predictably unable to suss out, but these events impressed upon me that the mind monster that hid among the cracks of my brain was clawing its way ever closer to the surface.

It was early afternoon, and me and Riles were waiting on Charlie. We had made it as far as Little Italy, and even this seemed a small miracle without the sage advice of our son turned urban sherpa. We settled down for some lunch and were served our meals by a gregarious man who looked like an extra plucked from the set of Goodfellas. He delighted in regaling us with tales about the old neighborhood and the history of the family-owned restaurant. We told him we had come from Nebraska, but we might as well have told him we fell down from the moon. In some way, the two of us, our lifestyle, was absolutely alien to him. Around this time, I noticed as he acted a bit more boisterous and his accent seemed to grow thicker. I suspected he was showing off, but it was all in good fun. We had a blast and our new friend, Antonio, called us by name any time he came to the table. It might sound corny, but for an hour, he made us feel like family.

"What's the matter? My cat can eat more than that," he said to me once I had given up on finishing my meatball sub.

"This thing's huge, man," I said.

"That's my grandmother's recipe," he said, rather dramatically. "If she thinks her cookin' wasn't good enough for you, well, let's just say, I wouldn't wanna be you."

"It was fantastic. You're fantastic. Your grandmother's fantastic. Italians are angels fell to earth," I said quickly, playing along and feigning fear. Okay, maybe I was actually a little afraid. "But I can't do no more."

"Alright, tell you what, I'll take care of it," Antonio said, rubbing his hands together and sounding like he had just agreed to help me hide a body.

"You're the man. Give grandma my best."

"Not a problem, not a problem. I'm just breaking your balls. Excuse me, honey, forgive my language," he said, looking over to Riley, who could not stop giggling. "I like youse. Fuhgeddaboudit, Paulie. Hey, even I have trouble getting to the last bite," he said in a whisper as he turned away with our plates.

"Hey, hey, hey," I shouted. "What did you call me?"

"Paulie. I was puttin' a little flair on your name. What's wrong with Paulie?" he asked, flatly, a bit put off after I had barked at him.

"Noth-nothing. I, hey, I'm sorry. That's, uh, that's not my name…" I trailed off and broke into a sweat. Antonio looked at me, puzzled, shrugged his shoulders, and disappeared into the kitchen.

"Dude, you okay?" Riley asked.

"What did he call me?" I asked her this and, as I did, I shuddered under a heavy sensation of fear. I knew full well what he had called me. I heard the word, clear as bells, but something about it didn't translate. I felt, in a sense, broken by an utterance of two syllables. I was honestly terrified. It seemed right plausible that my ability to understand language altogether was about to crack and splinter away.

"Paulie. He called you Paulie. So what?" she spoke to me calmly, but with worry in her voice.

"Excuse me," I mumbled, rising from the table.

The restaurant was small, but I was having a difficult time of navigating my way to the restroom. A fog had gripped me. The floor seemed to turn to silt. I couldn't plant a steady foot down as some cousin of vertigo went about bashing me around. I managed to stagger my way into a stall, fell to my knees, and puked into the toilet. As rivulets of vomit fell from my mouth, I began to cry. I had no idea why. This only served to heighten my sense of dread. I wept big tears, the kind reserved for moments of emotional anguish and pure terror.

After a few moments spent with my arms flung tightly

around a public toilet, I rose to my feet. I blew lines of snot from my nose and haphazardly splashed cold water onto my face. I straightened my clothes and tried my best to keep my red-rimmed eyes downturned as I exited the restroom. Riley had a look of panic on her face as she met me at the door. She grabbed my arm and led me out into the fresh air without saying a word.

We spent a few minutes on a bench. We sat in excruciating silence. We both made efforts not to look at the other. I'm sure our concerns were different, but each of us knew that what had happened was significant. But more than just that, what had taken place was dark.

"Riles, tell me again what he said," I whispered.

"Are you sure?" she asked, to which I just nodded. "Paulie."

I inhaled sharply, like I had just been stuck with a knife. I made her repeat the name a half dozen more times. I needed to steel myself against what it was about that sound that had troubled me so. I could sense that she hated this exercise. She was uncomfortable with it, upset, really. In a small way, in that moment, I felt that she was afraid of me.

Eventually we took to walking aimlessly. I suppose we only covered a few blocks, but what should have been a leisurely stroll felt to me like a march over rough terrain. We held hands but didn't say anything. Whatever sickness had just bored into me was something that neither of us wanted to address directly. With every step, I felt the tension mount. The squeeze of her hand was hard and her palm was sweaty. I knew we were both thinking the same thing. We were desperate to see Charlie, to be freed from this course that neither of us knew how to navigate. All of a sudden, New York City didn't seem so intimidating. It was what lived inside my shadow that was to be feared.

Charlie caught up with us, the day wound on, and my episode got lost in the busy day. Riley and me just kinda let it go without digging into it further. It was all we could do. I believe it was better that way. There are times when the best option left is to shut up and run in the other direction, so that's what we did. But what's the expression, you can run but you can't hide?

A little while later, we stopped in at Charlie's apartment. He weren't too keen on the idea, but Riles was insistent. I suppose her insistence was born from a mother's worry. She needed to see where her boy was living.

As Charlie had made abundantly clear, his place wasn't nothin' special. By New York standards, I guess it was an alright size, or, it would have been. The thing was, our boy shared this space with three others. They seemed to get along alright, though. They had something of a bohemian lifestyle going. I imagine that was the best solution for getting by. It seemed to be that the option was to either fully embrace the chaos and quirks that such living deals out or to be swallowed up by them. Hell, what did I care? I was just visiting and Charlie seemed rather pleased with his living situation. I can't say the same for his mom. She truly did love the madness of the big city, but I think a bit of a scare was put into her seeing her little boy placed at the center of the nonstop whirlwind of activity.

We sat around and chatted with a couple of the other fellas that lived there. It became clear pretty quick that this was to be a brief visit. There just wasn't space enough for all of us. It was kinda cool, the hour or so we spent at his place. It gave me a spell to rest my feet, as the long blocks of New York were working hell on my knees. This didn't seem the setting that would push me into another episode but, if there was one thing my scrambled brain was good at, it was in being unpredictable with its fits.

Riley was sitting with Charlie on an old loveseat. I had taken to lounging on the floor. An old Xbox was tucked into the corner, seemingly forgotten. I don't know why, but I picked up one of the controllers and started rolling it around in my hand. I took something of a fascination for the device and kinda fell away from everyone else for a time.

"Pistol whipped. Pistol whipped," I muttered to myself

while gazing into the controller like it was a crystal ball.

"Yo, Chuck, your old man's doing that MK flashback thing." One of his roommates, a guy they called Pickle, said this. He was a nice kid. A lanky bastard, and he was pure New York. He liked cracking wise more than Antonio and thought nothing of calling out a stranger for being strange.

The comment didn't register with me right away, but I picked up on the quiet that suddenly filled the room. I looked over to Riley, who by this point was staring daggers at Charlie's friend. Our boy jumped in pretty quick to lighten things up. He was a sharp kid and had a sense that one more weird comment was all it was going to take for Riley to unleash a dose of mama-bear rage. She was a pretty cool chick, but when it came to her children or my episodes, she became fiercely protective.

"Chill, mom, it's cool. He don't mean nothing by that," Charlie explained with a laugh. "It's kinda my fault, really. I might have told some people that papa P was part of the MK Ultra program," he explained, unable to suppress childish laughter.

"Is there anyone in this family that doesn't enjoy giving me a hard time?" I asked jokingly.

"Charlie, you're in college. And now, I'm having a hard time figuring out how that could have happened," said Riley with sarcasm, while looking into the air.

"Mom?"

"Because you're retarded," she said in that mom voice that can chill the blood of a grown man. "He's way too young to have been in MK Ultra. I thought that maybe you could do simple math. You know, with you being in college and all. I guess not."

"Aww, shit! Dude, your moms just called you retarded. Boom! I like her," said Pickle. He then made the mistake of pointing to Riley and winking.

"I will end you, Pickle," she said flatly. Everyone, including Pickle found this hilarious. Everyone, that is, except Riley. She just stared into that kid and I watched as he shrunk back into a child right before my eyes.

"Sorry, ma'am," said Pickle.

"What kinda name is Pickle anyway?" she asked, incredulously.

"It's uh, it's not my real name."

"Mom, look at his nose," said Charlie.

"Charlie, Christ, don't be mean. Pickle, don't listen to him," said Riley.

"Okay, now I'm really confused. You were just yelling at me a second ago," Pickle said.

"I didn't raise him to be mean. Besides, I can yell at the both of you. And, see these?" asked Riley as she shook her hands out in front of her. "I have two hands, I can slap the both of you. Behave." She really tried to keep the fear going, but her playful nature betrayed her as a smile wiggled across her face.

"Hey, Pickle," I said. "What else did Charlie tell you about me?"

"Oh, Paul, don't encourage this crap."

"Why not? This is fun," I said.

"It's not funny," Riley said quietly, obviously thinking about what had happened earlier in the restaurant.

"C'mon, Pickle, out with it," I coaxed.

"Mom, papa P, the thing is, I kinda tell everyone a different story. Sorry if that's not cool. I wasn't really thinking," said Charlie.

"Charlie, I don't mind. I'd probably do the same thing in your place. Shit, I might start doing that anyway. Hey, what can I say, it's a good idea," I said, to which Riley groaned.

"So, should I go ahead?" asked Pickle shyly.

"Sure, whatever," said Riley, relenting. "But if you've told anyone that he used to star in porn just omit that for me, please."

"Okay, so Chuckles told me that he was in MK Ultra, you know? He told Lance, you guys don't know him-"

"No shit, Pickle, go on," Riley said.

"Yeah, anyway, so he told Lance that Paul was an assassin.

Like a James Bond kinda dude. I heard him once say that Paul was a former Yakuza boss. Hey, I know that don't make sense, but that one's a pretty good story. Oh, and he told Shelley that Paul worked on the Manhattan Project. She's dumb, she bought it."

Riley rubbed her forehead. I think she was going to give them another math lesson about how me being involved with the Manhattan Project was actually impossible. She probably wanted to get to the bottom of whoever Shelley was, but she just let it all go. I was addressing my ghosts and having a good time doing so. Charlie was visibly glad to be back in his mother's company. Pickle, well, he, for all his questionable manners, was just too likeable to resist. Riley gave in and laughed with the rest of us, allowing herself to enjoy the absurdity of the whole situation.

After that exchange, we all got to having a good time. I felt the desire to linger longer, but Charlie had some other obligations that required his attention. That was too bad. I felt the urge to hook up that Xbox to try and figure out if playing a few games might trigger anything else. For the first time, I grew curious of the meanings to the things hidden within me. I felt light, relieved, I guess, as I considered that maybe as a child, I had a friend who called me Paulie and regularly handed me my ass at video games. The notion was pleasant and silly. It demystified my demons and cut them down to size. It made me think that, even though my episodes came at me harsh and visceral, maybe my reactions were just mixed up. Perhaps I was getting myself all worked up over nothing. Maybe, in the way-back, I was really just some ordinary boring guy. There was something about reflexively uttering the phrase *pistol whipped*, though, that continued to needle me. We were on vacation. I let it go. After all, my demons might have been diminished, but they were still demons all the same. I figured it best to let them sleep for as long as I could.

12. Cracks In The Ice

By the time we arrived back in Nebraska, I was good and ready for the quiet and slow pace of the Midwest. On the plane for our return trip, I grew antsy to go home. It was then that I came to realize something. At long last, there was a place that I felt I belonged. *Home* was no longer another word that I used to vaguely describe the place where I fell into sleep. It had come to mean so much more. Back then, and maybe even still, I never felt that I was from a particular place. There wasn't anything that seemed to tie me to one portion of the country or another, but on that day, I knew where home was, and it felt incredible.

Hannah was getting set to strike out for herself. Riley was fully aware of this before we sauntered off to New York but, once we were back, the reality of the situation came for her. She kept up a strong demeanor around her little girl but I imagined that even Hannah could see that Riles was having a rough go with it all. Maybe without the kids in the house, she was afraid that her role of mom would somehow ebb away. Maybe with them gone she would feel old. I don't know. It wasn't my struggle to understand. The funny thing about Hannah leaving, though? She didn't go far. I think it was all more or less that the years had gone on, and the kids, well, they were kids no more.

Ever the tomboy, Hannah went into the welding trade. As part of her training, she scooted around Nebraska and the neighboring states doing jobs to hone her skills. She was even part of a team that spent near a month down in Texas. She would stay at the house from time to time but her main place of residence was in Omaha. It made sense. There were more opportunities for her in and around the city. When she couldn't make it back home during her time off, me and Riley would pack up the car and head over to spend time with Hannah. We made the trip close to once a month for a while. Eventually, the gap between trips grew wider, but that was just the natural order of things.

Hannah was Independent and tough, and so I never held

much worry over her being flung out into parts unknown, but even I took a measure of comfort once she got herself established. She landed a gig as an industrial pipe welder. She was in a union, making a good wage, and secured herself the promise of steady employment.

Hannah hadn't been in Omaha for long when she moved in with her boyfriend, Andy. The move surprised everyone, probably even Hannah herself. She was never one to keep a guy around for too long. By the time she was old enough to take an interest in boys, she swore that she'd never permanently attach herself to anyone. That all just sounded too boring for her. I had always suspected that there was more of feisty Aunt Julia in her than she let her mother see. I think settling down and domesticity had long been undesirable notions to her.

It was funny watching Riley quietly fuss over Hannah when she was exploring the merits of a polyamorous lifestyle. That was the tasteful spin that Riles chose to put on it, anyway. Most folks have another name for the way in which Hannah conducted herself regarding the company of the opposite sex, but fuck those people. From where I stood, Hannah was happy, and that was all that mattered. But the universe has quite the penchant for toying around with its playthings. Because, once Hannah hooked up with Andy, her mother's concerns shifted. Riley was made to reflect on her own choices made during the spontaneity of youth. It seemed that once Hannah stopped moving too fast, she was in danger of moving too slow. But we all got our lessons to learn, and there ain't no guide for how to go about living. Hannah could be something of a force of nature, and that girl loved her freedom, but it's love that can alter every aspect of how someone looks at the world.

She and Andy gave us the news of their plan to cohabitate one spring evening around the dinner table of her childhood home. She seemed somewhat hesitant to tell me and her mom, but there was never a need for worry. We both liked Andy. He was the typical all-American Midwestern boy. He was polite, charming, and had an affection for Hannah that rivaled my own feelings for Riley. He was almost too nice, delicate even. It's a wonder that she kept him around. Usually guys like him slipped under her radar. I felt happy for Andy. He was that rare everyman that got lucky. He struck me as the type that had always aimed for the stars, pining for girls that were out of his league. But, hell, there he was, the genuine good man who had nabbed a truly wonderful woman that also just so happened to be out of his league.

Of course, the evening wasn't all feel-good tales peppered with sunny predictions for the future. Julia was there, after all, and she put that poor bastard through the grinder. I'm sure his better half had done her best to prepare him for the skewering to come, but until a grizzly bear actually sinks its teeth into the skin, it's hard to properly grasp the concept of what it means to be bitten.

I must admit, I enjoyed this part of the evening a whole lot more than I probably should have. It was interesting for me. Shit, if I'm honest, it was fun for me, being a spectator to the ire of Julia rather than its target. Gleefully, I watched Andy grow desperate under this impromptu interrogation. He would look to Riley, then over to Hannah, hoping, pleading, it seemed, for one of them to swoop in and rescue him. He had taken to avoiding my gaze. As we gathered in the dining room, I had positioned myself behind Julia. From this vantage I went about making faces and giving the finger to the back of Julia's head. Riles and her daughter kept straight faces and mostly ignored my behavior, but Andy made the mistake of laughing during the early goings. Little did he know that such levity acted as an invitation to his diminutive oppressor to bring about more quills. Welcome to the family, kid.

After the meal and subsequent inquisition, Andy popped out back. He said he wanted some fresh air and, being more or less a city boy, wanted to take in the countryside at dusk. That was some first-class bullshit. What he really wanted was some distance between himself and Julia. Hannah got nervous and complained to her mom, Julia didn't see what the fuss was all about, and I grabbed a couple of beers from the fridge.

"Here, kid, have a beer," I said, once I found Andy wandering about aimlessly out back.

"No, thanks. I don't drink very much," he said quietly.

"Oh, you will. Trust me. I've spent so much time around that harpy in there that it's a wonder I ain't smokin' meth just to take the edge off."

"Thanks," he said with a chuckle, taking one of the bottles from my hand.

He twisted off the cap and proceeded to take slow and regular sips. He pretended to study things gone dark off in the distance and kept a few paces away from me as we milled around the yard. He avoided my gaze and took no initiative to engage me in conversation.

"Hey, man, relax," I said finally. "I ain't gonna give you the speech about *if you mistreat my little girl, I'm gonna bury you in the back yard*. I mean, I will, but that's neither here nor there. And besides, it ain't me you need to worry about. Lighten up. From what I see and from what Hannah says, you're a good dude. You guys seem happy, and you got the stamp of approval from Riley. You're fine," I said, and gave Andy a pat on the shoulder.

"Is she always like that, Hannah's aunt?" he asked, exasperated, but with a little life in his voice.

"I'd like to tell you no, but I'd be lying. She's a lot to take in but, and it pains me to say this, Julia's a really cool chick. You just gotta brave the first meeting, and the one after that, and the one after that. You get the idea. But underneath it all, she can be pretty sweet."

"She sure has a funny way of showing it," said Andy.

"You don't wanna know the worst of it," I said.

"Oh?"

"The shit she was giving you at dinner? That was her taking to you. Now just imagine how that would have went had she deemed you unworthy," I said, raising my hands to the sky as to mock Julia's god complex.

Andy shuddered comedically, we both got a laugh and then he said, "Mr. Parker, sir, can I ask you something?"

"Okay, just knock off the mister and sir stuff. It's Paul, alright."

"Sorry," he said, sheepishly.

"Go on, shoot. What did you want to ask me?" I said.

"Is it true that you don't know where you came from?"

"Whoa, Andy! From quiet and reserved to asking the tough questions," I said.

"I don't mean to pry. I'm just very interested in some of the things that Hannah's told me about you. I remember hearing your story when I was younger. It always fascinated me."

"I don't mind. My past is the first thing people want to ask me about. Hell, sometimes it's the only thing they want to ask me about. Funny thing is, though, most folks never work up the nerve to do it. So, to answer your question, no, I don't know where I came from. It goes a bit deeper than all that, too. I don't have a damned idea about what I did with the first twenty years of my life," I said with a shrug.

"That must be so strange," Andy said, mostly to himself, and then sipped his beer.

"To tell you the truth, I don't think on it much," I said.

"Has anything ever come back to you after all this time?"

"How serious are you about Hannah?" I said quickly, abruptly shifting gears.

"Sir? Sorry, Paul, what do you mean by that?" asked Andy. I could tell as nervousness crept back into him from being put on the spot.

"Just answer the question. It should be pretty easy."

"I love her," he said directly. "I know the time isn't quite right yet, but I want to ask her to marry me. Sometime soon, I hope. She's amazing. She just makes every part of my life better."

"Okay, fair enough. That's pretty big. I'm guessin' you ain't told that to too many people?" I asked.

"I haven't told anyone."

"Well then, I'll tell you something that no one else knows. Call it a bonding-type thing, with us hopefully going to be family and all one day. I have dreams, sometimes, where I see things that might be memories, but I don't really put much stock in what I see when I'm asleep. I do have one memory, though, a real one. I'm standing in a living room, and there's others standing around with me. We're all wearing party masks or something, dime-store kinda shit. Anyway, there's people seated on a couch, three of 'em. Maybe a family. There's a man and a woman, and a girl that seems high-school age. It's weird, though. None of them are wearing masks and they ain't saying nothing. Hell, they ain't even moving. It's like they're scared. That's about it, but I can't figure its meaning. I don't know if it's a surprise party gone wrong or maybe a bad practical joke. Whatever it is, it's just plain weird. So, what do ya think of that?" I asked.

Andy thought a moment, finished off his drink and then started laughing. "Oh my god," he said, chuckling.

"What? Out with it."

"Paul, I'm thinking maybe you were one of those really bad party acts. Like a cheap rent-a-clown."

"Aww, come on man. Is that the best you can do?" I asked.

"No, listen. My mom and dad have always been weird, like naïve, I guess. Anyway, when my sister was sixteen, I think, they had something like that show up to the house for her birthday. It was some entertainment troupe that normally comes to birthday parties for little kids. They were totally uncomfortable with the whole thing, my sister was pissed, and my parents were oblivious to how awkward the situation really was. I thought it was hilarious. I still make fun of her for it. I hate to tell you, but I think that's what you did before," Andy finished off his assessment of me by laughing some more.

"I'm regretting coming out here to cheer you up," I said, dryly.

"No worries. Your secret's safe with me. Although it might kill me not to tell Hannah about this."

"I bet it would make her smile," I said, but mostly to myself. "I'll tell you what. You can tell Hannah, but never, ever tell Julia. We got a deal?" I asked.

"Deal," said Andy, as he shook my hand.

"That don't sound so bad, anyway," I said after a time, laughing at the idea of my presumed former occupation. "Besides, I could have been a lot worse."

13. Our Time

By the time that me and Riles had been together for ten years the time finally arrived for us to focus primarily on each other. The kids were off doing their things and living their lives. Blaine and his new brood were little more than distant memories. Riley's parents kept themselves busy and, as such, hadn't popped in for a visit in some time. They had always been a strong presence in our lives and I was ever grateful for it, but their absence around this time came as something of a blessing. It was as if, in the wisdom gained from decades of marital experience, they knew that Riley and me needed nothing more than to truly be with one another. For the first time we would have unfiltered access to each other, to discover the personal aspects that had for so long lain dormant under blankets of day-to-day obligations to others.

To celebrate the milestone of our tin anniversary, me and my girl cashed in some vacation time. It would seem reasonable that we set off to an exotic locale or booked a trip to the Grand Canyon. I'm sure that would've been nice. In years past we had taken such trips. We'd packed up the kids and went to the beach. We'd embarked on back-country road trips to nose around musty junk shops and charming antique stores. We had enjoyed wandering around eccentric small towns to take in the local color. But for this occasion, we did none of that. No, for the better part of two weeks, we just bummed around Stone Horse.

I know that must sound a bit strange. After all, a well-planned ten minutes is enough time to see a visitor to most of the highlights on offer in Stone Horse. We were residents. There wasn't a thing to do that we both hadn't done a hundred times over, but that was the point. This time wasn't about trips or plans or exploration. It was about us, for us. We passed the days doing seemingly forgettable and inane things that we hadn't thought to do in years. It made us feel young. It reminded us of why we came together all those years ago. The simple truth of the matter was that all either of us really needed was the person who occupied the other side of the bed at night. It was kinda like, after all the noise and chaos of regular life, we came to remember just how much we loved each other.

In the years that followed, we continued the establishment of *us*. We made new friends. We whiled away weekend evenings shooting pool down at Dusty's Tavern and regressed back to a time that neither of us got to share in before. Like teenagers exploring romance for the first time, we went to outdoor rock concerts and made out in the grass of the lawn section. We went to amusement parks and screamed like idiots as our bodies were tussled about by roller coasters both of us were growing too old to properly handle. One night, Riley brought home a dime bag of pot. We smoked ourselves stupid and, later in the evening, we snuck into a movie theater. Money wasn't an issue, and I can't recall what was screening, but it was fun.

My old nemesis, Julia, had just tripped her way over forty and moved in with what had to be one of the most patient men ever to walk the earth. I came to suspect that she was going through something of a mid-life crisis. Her man, Roger, was precisely the type she once would have shredded. He was a craft beer enthusiast, wore a man-bun, and was a pacifist. He was a hell of a guy, and quite the cut-up, but how a fellow like that ended up with the Midwest's answer to Medusa is a riddle that will forever vex me.

The four of us made for quite the team and took to palling around whenever schedules would allow. It was the start of summer, as best as I can remember, that me, Riles, her sister, and Roger scooted on down to New Orleans for a long weekend of foolishness and excess.

Ever since I had assumed the identity of Paul Parker, I wasn't one to take to drink. I had no desire for late nights filled with noise and excitement. I preferred the quiet. I liked to simply exist among the natural sounds of the world around me. I suppose I shifted into the role of background player upon the stage of life. That may sound rather dull, but it was precisely this type of existence that made me feel happy and safe. This is part of why Riles made for such a great match for me. Together, we eschewed the haste that seemed to grip so many others in a never-ending and futile pursuit for happiness through constant motion. We were content just to stand still, so long as the other was standing by.

With all that being said, a stopover into all the mad activity that New Orleans can host was a good experience for us. We continued our masquerade as young lovers as we unburdened ourselves of inhibition and reservation. During our time in The Big Easy, we stayed up to greet the rising of the sun, got drunk before the clock lumbered its way to the strike of noon, and danced with strangers on the streets.

Even at middle age, Julia fell right into her element. She dragged the rest of us along, caught in the wake of her inexhaustible energy. Roger received a swift lesson in what it means to keep up with her but, to his credit, he proved to be fit to the task. At times tired and obviously overwhelmed, he seemed to genuinely relish every moment of the frantic pace we kept. There seemed no annoyance that could crack his calm disposition, and he gazed with boyish wonder at all the things rarely glimpsed back in the Midwest.

Roger proved to be something of a stabilizing force to me. When I was falling back or ready to leave behind all the lights and sounds of the city, he would coax me on. He had that magic about him. It took just a few words uttered in his quirky voice, and I was back on board, ready for more. He became the support I needed as Riley teamed up with her little sister during most of the nights we spent out on the town. Julia was quick to spot the shift in Riley's character, and she was even quicker to prod her elder sibling into more outrageous behavior. I must say, it was pricelessly adorable watching Riles oscillate from good country girl to wild party chick. After a while, she began to play up the persona of wide-eyed good girl looking for any excuse to cut loose.

Age was taking its time putting its stamp on Riles. To me, she still looked every bit as youthful as she did when we met all those years ago. Maybe it was for this reason that she took so easily to the antics of a college kid turned loose for spring break. I don't know, but I knew she was having the time of her life. While we were there, her smile never left her face and laughter was ever-present in her throat. For the first time, I genuinely could say that I loved Julia. She had a way of stripping away all the bullshit that makes so many of us scared. She definitely made the trip better and dug a sense of unbridled fun from Riley that I could never quite manage to do. I'll be forever grateful to her for that.

"Oh my god, dude," Riley said to me during the waning hours of our last night in New Orleans. She was sitting on the hotel bed, her legs tucked under her, giggling hysterically as she clutched a handful of beads. "What the hell did I do?"

"You flashed your titties to a bunch of strangers," I answered, amused.

"Ugh, that probably wasn't necessary, was it?" she asked, falling back into the bed.

"No, probably not. You could have just bought some beads, I imagine."

"Damnit, Julia!" she said, laughter still in her voice.

"Did you have fun, though?" I asked.

"Shit yeah, man," she said.

"I was saving this for the last night, so here goes. You don't remember almost getting arrested, do you?" I asked, and watched as her eyes got big.

"Uh, no, but I think I'd remember that. Are you fucking with me?" she asked, genuinely confused.

"Nope. We were at that corner bar, the one with the dressed-up skeletons painted on the doors to the bathrooms. You had like ten screwdrivers and for some reason decided to try smoking. You wandered outside to bum cigarettes. Is this ringing any bells?" I asked.

"Kinda," she said nervously, biting her nails.

"So, you asked some dude for a smoke. He asked to see your boobs. He wasn't even being serious, but before he could pull out his pack, you just whipped them out."

"Oh no!" she said and buried her face with a pillow.

"Oh yes, and the cop that was standing next to you wasn't too amused," I said, to which she gasped. "I guess he had his fill of dealing with drunks for the night, 'cause he was ready to cuff you right there." I could barely keep from laughing at this point. Riley didn't think it was all that funny and took to throwing pillows at me.

"Jesus Christ, I barely remember that. So, what happened?" she asked.

"Roger," was all I said.

"What? Roger? What did he do?"

"What he always does, being that calming force. I don't know how he did it, I was too busy tryin' to keep you contained, but he talked the cop down," I explained.

"That guy is a saint. Hey?" she said, changing gears a bit. "What was Julia doing while all this was going on?"

"Laughing at your dumb ass," I said.

"That bitch!"

"Here, check this out," I said, passing Riles a sheet of paper.

Late one night when we were all good and tuned up, Julia had shoved Riley into one of those novelty photo booths where different backgrounds and texts can be added to the pictures. Jules only choose to save one, but it was a close up of her and Riley, both with eyes half closed and makeup smeared. Riley especially looked every bit the haggard tourist put through the wringer of a city known for alcohol and partying.

"Cougars gone wild," she whispered to herself as she read the tag at the bottom of the picture. "Ugh, I love that girl," said Riley, as a grin again found her lips.

14. Sun And Snow

Like everyone who has ever lived, or ever will live, me and Riley came to confront our own challenges. Storms blew our way and were summarily weathered. Obstacles, some of daunting proportion, were placed in our path, but we always managed to find a way 'round. However, neither of us were prepared to battle the next misfortune that circumstance saw fit to rifle our way.

It wasn't long after we had arrived back from our trip to Louisiana that Julia took sick. Six months later, we put her in the ground. Cancer came for her and its march through her body was swift and merciless. To me, it wasn't the death that shook me so much as it was the dying. To watch what that disease can do, the way it goes about dismantling someone, is overwhelming. What happened to Julia wasn't merely illness, it was the methodic and total erasure of a person.

Every day, that sickness took a little more from her. Seemingly, she weighed less by the hour. Her color faded, and with its recession came the certainty that it would never return. Her wit dulled, and her speech slowed and softened to a whisper most days. Finally, the fight left her eyes. That was the worst part. I never could have imagined a woman so vibrant, an individual that burned like an atomic ray, left with nothing but quiet defeat. Julia was one of those people who seemed capable of surviving the cockroaches and the end times, and then she was just gone. It broke my heart, but it did worse to Riley.

Cancer may have taken Julia in totality, but before it had finished with her, it bit away chunks from her sister. Its damage left wounds never to heal. It permanently fractured the most important person in my life, and there was nothing I could do. Helplessly, I watched Riles as she fell apart.

She didn't immediately slip under waves of grief. That was to come later. For a while, her mood was buoyed by all the activity that the house hosted just after Julia's passing. Her parents and the kids flew in and all stayed at our place for the better part of a week. The house was full, and the air danced with warm anecdotes about the exploits and eccentricities of the dearly departed. Soon enough though, everyone left. In the wake of their leaving came the silence and the tears. The sleepless nights and the listlessness that loss employs to numb the spirit.

"I wanna be serious with you for a second, for once. Fuck, it'll probably be for the last time," Julia had said to me, meekly, as she lay dying in her hospital bed. "You're the best thing that has ever happened to Riley, I hope you know that. Take care of her, okay?"

I put my hand on her knee but said nothing. I turned my head away, trying to hide the arrival of tears. I listened to the beeps and hum of the machines and thought about how the glare of fluorescent light seemed cruel. Its glow was generic and sterile in the worst sense. It would be better to simply die in the dark. I collected myself and rose. With one last squeeze placed on her hand, I made for the door.

"Hey, Paul," she called out before I slipped out the door. "Eat a dick, homo."

I looked back. She had raised her middle finger to me. Her hand was sallow and thin, her bald head was wrapped up in a bandana. Although the skin upon her face was sunken, that telltale grin hid in the corner of her mouth. I smiled back, turned away, and cried.

It seemed fitting for Julia to go out with an insult on her lips. She was supposed to have roughly a week left, but as the quirks of fate would have it, she died later that day. I was the last person to see her alive. I'm not sure how that makes me feel. I debated the fairness of it, but was made to conclude that fairness had left Jules behind a long time ago. I thought about crafting something poetic when Riley asked me to relay to her the last words of her sister. I deemed it better to tell the truth. In what would become a rare occurrence for a long time to follow, I saw Riley smile.

About a week after the funeral, me and Riley went to visit Julia's grave. It felt to me a curious and toxic exercise. There could be nothing gained by such and act. Words uttered to a cold stone would bring no sense of closure. Closure is something that I've learned is at best a fairytale, and at worst a farcical and torturous concept. It is an invention crafted by those who have never felt the need for it.

We were warmed under the sunshine of an early winter's day, but I still felt nothing but cold. As we stood in silent rigidity, I watched the snow as it fell over the graves. These forces made me think of Julia, and they made me angry. Like the sun, she once burned bright and her presence was undeniable. But then, and forevermore, she was like the snow that melted into the ground, cold and absorbed into earth. I took Riley's hand in mine but didn't speak. We hadn't talked during the short drive to the cemetery and continued on in silence. We exchanged no words as we made for home, and went to sleep that night without a sound directed toward the other. For Riley, the pain was too intense to be given voice.

15. Coming Undone

An uncomfortable silence fell over our house. It's strange how devastating something invisible, something so hollow, like the absence of sound, can be. This was not a horrid time. It was just one without color. Joy receded from our lives and all that was left was gray.

It took, as best as I can remember, nearly two years before Riley came out of the shadows cast by her sister's passing. I did what I could, or what I thought needed done to make things easier on Riles. As malaise paralyzed her, I tended to the everyday tasks that she normally handled. And, at times, I simply stayed distant, as the grief that enveloped her caused her to withdraw.

In those days, there was so much pain. It was anguish mixed up with the uncertainty of what next to do and worry over what was to come. But, like the earth as it inevitably turns again to face the sun, light made its way back into our lives. My spirits were lifted, and my heart was made lighter with every step Riley took back to herself, even if these steps came slowly. At long last, she came to terms with what had happened. I won't say that everything returned to normal, for after such a subtraction, a return to things as they once were isn't truly attainable, but healing eventually came.

As our shared despair began to recede, love again became the dominant force in our relationship. It was these years, the final years I spent with Riley, that have served to cut me the deepest. There was rarely anything of note that took place, but that was the sweetness of it all. Her parents were happy with their new lives. The children were successful and had each found satisfaction in their endeavors. Our concerns were few, a bright and welcoming future seemingly ahead of us.

Although I had consistently played down my feelings over the past I could no longer remember, the unknown had always needled me. It was there, ever present, in the back of my mind. The wondering had never left me and, then, one day, the questions saw fit to take their leave of my thoughts. The bad dreams I sometimes had drifted off, the episodes I suffered ceased. They seemed like echoes that had finally faded. This seemed to me to be the completion of the forgetting of my former life. I didn't know what I was rid of, but I was glad for its dissipation.

It was all there, the years ahead, the privilege of traveling into the depths of old age with the love of my life. The struggles of raising another man's children were past. The days of anxiety over making ends meet were gone. The trials and traps set to test the bond forged between Riley and myself had been bested and it seemed that the best was yet to come. That was the script, the way it was supposed to go. It was the way I wanted it to go. But in the salvage yard of our wants and dreams can be found the reality, the unflinching callousness, of life.

I was alone, out back, aimlessly walking the yard during a cool morning in spring. Simple and bullshit trivialities occupied my thoughts: where to put the new shed, thin patches of grass that would need seeded. There was dew on the blades that folded under my step and a hazy mist floated around me and encircled the trees. I can't recall how I felt in that moment, or if I felt anything at all. But it was in this almost meditative state that my memories saw fit to fill me with feeling. When it all came down or, rather, when it all came back, it was as if everything I had been for the past twenty years was blinked from existence.

I buckled and fell to my knees in the wet grass. A great sense of weight impressed itself upon me as I suffered the visions of all my memories once misplaced. What afflicted me was like an inverted purge. The sensation pummeled me, but I can't remember having much of a physical response to the distress I felt. It was as if I was stunned, stricken by a paralysis and a wakefulness that forced me to acknowledge the creature I used to be. The images of my past bored through my mind with a ferocious clarity. The things that I remembered, I could not accept, yet this was a truth I could not deny.

I returned to the house and collapsed into a chair. I sat in the kitchen and looked around. I felt like a stranger in another's home. Silently, I criticized the loose boards of the hardwood floor and the chipped plaster ceiling. I noticed the drip of the faucet. It never bothered me before. Now, it was practically infuriating. Bands of sunlight fell over me, but I felt no warmth. I grew uncomfortable and felt woefully out of place. I began to despise myself. Looking about at all the shit that needed fixin' made me realize what a disappointment I must have been to Riley all these long years. I, Paul Parker, was a weight she never cut loose. Paul Parker, what a ridiculous concept. Immediately, I came to view my masquerade as pathetic and absurd.

In my mind, a war was being waged between two personalities. I thought of Riley, and my heart broke. I felt cheated, betrayed by some cruelty of the cosmos. But, more than all that, I took to thoughts of revenge. I saw Wayne, Bill, and Polly as clear as day. They were what really occupied my thinking. It struck me how quickly the imposter was forced from my being as Kellen Black assumed his rightful place inside my mind.

Maybe it was the years I had spent away from him. Maybe it was all the time I went about pretending to be a man and not a beast. Perhaps it was all the love others had graciously sent my way since my arrival in Nebraska. I don't know. But, whatever the reasons, Kellen wasn't permitted a full return. Oh, I knew what needed doing, but my focus was straightened. I felt no more desire to hurt the innocent, to steal and to destroy. But I harbored a wrath within me. It was a righteous fury, or so I told myself. Polly and the other architects of my disposal were out there, somewhere, walking the earth. This I could not abide. It was then that I resolved to do the hardest thing I would ever undertake. I would leave Riley.

I spent the remainder of the day steeling myself for the conversation to come. I carved away some time to think of the kids and, in the quiet of my mind, to bid them farewell. They were grown adults, and I knew to leave them was to be a coward, but I saw no other way. The role of a parent is to shield those in their care from the claws of monsters. What I had been, what I had done, those acts confirmed for me that I no longer deserved their love. This also assured me that they were better off far from my presence.

I ran my mind around in circles trying to justify what all this would mean for Riley. I thought of all the promises I had once made to her that I would shatter by leaving. However, with all things considered, she was much too special for me. Inevitably, as Kellen, I would only serve to poison her. She was the light, the stars, and the shimmering sea. I was the mud and the muck. To stay would only be to defile and tarnish her. She deserved better than I could ever hope to achieve. There was too much back there on the dirty road of my past. It was too late for me, and, in a moment of naked introspection, I acknowledged that I didn't deserve no peace. How could I stay? How could I continue this pantomime, this comfortable and fulfilling life, when I had damaged the lives of so many others? Just like Wayne, just like Bill, just like Polly, I had my own bill comin' due.

Night came down and I knew no rest. I was grateful that Riles was off visiting Hannah for the weekend. It gave me time to plan and to plot. I may have frittered away the day ping-ponging between feelings of anger and self-pity, but all that was coming to a close. For the duration of the sleepless hours that followed, I went about putting my affairs in order. I got myself a scheme worked out and settled on a starting point. Now, it could be suggested that I made myself too busy for sorrow, but I don't think that's accurate. See, all throughout this time, I never once broke down. I didn't shed a tear. This callousness, this dearth of emotion, illuminated the fact that Paul was dying, maybe dead already. There was only one path left to me. I gave serious consideration to fleeing under the dark of night, to leaving my Riley with nothing but questions. I had almost worked myself up to this savage act of cowardice when I heard the familiar rattle of the knob on our front door.

The door creaked open and it snapped me from the trance I had been locked inside for the better part of two days. I was on the couch, my nose in the laptop. I quickly cleared the history and smacked it shut. Riley tossed her keys onto an end table and wandered into the room. I imagine she said something to me. I'm sure it was sweet and delivered in her bubbly tone, but whatever it might have been, it escaped my ears. From the corner of my eye, I noticed as she came upon me. Her arrival was quick and then halted. She seemed to creep slowly towards me, realizing that something had changed. In twenty years' time, I was never cold to her. Then, I was as distant to her as the darkest reaches to be found at the bottom of the sea. I couldn't bring myself to look at her. I was afraid that my nerve would crack and she would then spend the rest of her life with a beast. However unlikely it seemed, I was concerned that I might harm her. That was just the way of things for Kellen, for me, to take the quickest path through any situation. I just wanted it over.

"Paul, what's wrong?" she asked, with more worry in her voice than I had ever heard before. It was then that I looked up, and she had her answer.

"How, how much did you remember?" she asked, nervously. "Honey, whatever it is, we can get through this."

"I remember it all, Riles," I said softly.

"Okay, great, right?" she said, and exhaled sharply.

"I've been dreading this day for twenty years. As it turns out, I had good reason."

"Paul, baby, listen to me," she began, sitting beside me and taking my hand in hers. "Whatever this means, it doesn't matter. Nothing changes. We can get through this. There's nothing to be afraid of."

"I ain't scared, Riley. I'm leaving," I said as I rose from my seat.

"What?" she asked, reflexively shaking her head in confusion. "Leaving? Where are you going? I, I don't understand."

"It's just the way it's gotta be. There's something I need to finish," I said.

"Paul, you need to tell me what's going on," she said, toughening her tone.

"My name's Kellen. I'm not a nice man, Riles. I need to leave. You need me gone. There's shit I got to do. That's just the way it is. Deal with it however you have to," I said.

"No, no. You don't get to do this. You've spent half your life with me and, unless you've been full of shit for the last twenty years, this is the only half that matters to you. So, no,

I'm not just going to deal with it and you're not leaving. Just listen to yourself. I need you gone? Fuck you. I need *you*, Paul. Now tell me what is going on so we can figure out how to fix this," she said, her arms crossed, tears now upon her cheeks.

"I've killed people. Does that change anything?" I said. I put my hand out in front of me as she went to speak and then went on. "Well, I can't say that for sure, but only because after I got done beating someone down, I just bailed. I didn't run because I was thinking about getting caught, I just didn't care."

"No, no, no, no," she said. "No, it doesn't change anything. Go to fucking confession, see a therapist." There was more she was trying to say, but the weight of what I had said momentarily silenced her.

"I'm a rapist."

"Fuck you," was her reply. It came with an exasperated laugh. "Just cut the bullshit. Who is she?" Riley asked after a long pause.

"This ain't about another woman. I wouldn't do that to you."

"Oh, that's so thoughtful. But you'd leave? Seriously, what is this? If you want out, go, but don't make me out to be a fucking idiot," she said.

"I don't wanna go. I wish it didn't have to be like this. Riley, I love you, always will," I said, finding the composure to soften my voice.

"Then I guess you are leaving. Everyone who says they love me ends up leaving," she said to herself in a whisper.

"You ain't seeing this for what it is," I started, but was cut off by her.

"What about Hannah and Charlie? They call you *dad*. Are you just going to run out on them too? What's the matter with you?"

"Goddamn it, Riley, you're not listening," I said, raising my voice to her for probably the first time in our relationship. "By going, I'm trying to protect them, and you, from me. I used to do home invasions. I terrorized people's children. Killed their pets. Everything I said to you is true. Now, you really want to sleep next to me?"

"Okay, okay," she said, pulling herself together. "How do you know that what you remember is true? Maybe you just had a really bad, really vivid episode. I can't know how scary this must be, just, please, try to be calm. Listen to me, everything will be okay."

"You don't have to go outside when it's raining to know you're gonna get wet. You know why? Because it's all come down on you before. It's undeniable. It's the truth. It's like that for me. This ain't no episode. What I'm telling you is real, and I gotta go. That's the end of it, Riles," I explained. For the first time in our conversation, tears broke from my eyes. It was only for a moment, and I kept myself a distance from her. I couldn't go near her. There was no going back for me. There was no use in trying to fool myself otherwise.

"I don't believe you. I can't believe you," she said defensively, but her resolve was cracking as the impact of my revelations were settling into her.

It was then, looking at her, admiring her one last time, I guess, that I saw it: the fear in her eyes. Somewhere deep inside, she knew that what I was saying was true. It was hard to swallow, but just a taste of who I really am was in her mouth. She was afraid of me and she looked to me, finally, as aged, old. In two months' time she was going to turn fifty-four, but in just these last few moments, I put more age on her than nature ever could. I was killing her. The shame and agony that fell upon me were overwhelming. It hurt me more than any beating or betrayal ever did. My old favorite companion, pain, had returned, but I no longer desired its company. But my wants and needs were of no consequence. The pain was here to stay.

For all of that, though, there was one thing in particular that told me it was time to go. It was the way Riley looked at me. It wouldn't be detectable all the time, but damn sure it would be there. We could go forward and pretend. She could try and deny my true self, and I could fool myself into believing that I could hide it from her. But none of that was going to happen. To see the way she looked at me then, was something I could not bear. Furthermore, if I stuck around, that brokenhearted stare would linger behind her eyes until she shut them in death. And, if I stuck around, I knew she would endure it. Maybe it ain't right, but to me, leaving seemed the only option I had left to save her.

"Paul," she said to me softly. "I love you with all my heart, and I know the man that you are. You're a good man. You can go on being that man. Please, please don't do this to me," she pleaded.

"I done worse," I said, as I opened the door and walked out into the night.

Chapter Three: Sometimes, The Only Thing Left To Build Is A Fire

16. Division

Paul Parker was dead. I knew that the moment I walked out of the house and into the night. He was gone, but his ghost remained. His specter took to following me around and its influence helped set me to purpose. I knew the things ahead of me. They would require the touch of Kellen to see through to completion. But I didn't want to be Kellen again, not fully. I needed those traces of Paul to keep me right, to keep me on the path. Most of all, I suppose, I needed him to stand as a barrier between me and the innocents I was to come across. They had no part to play in all this, and I resolved to do them no harm. As it were, though, the wishes of the dead always lose out to the desires of the living. As such, I knew that the ghost I carried would have his say, but I also knew the time would come when I would have to ignore his pleas.

In all my years spent with Riley, I was only dishonest to her once. This act of deceit began early and my intentions were noble enough to justify the trickery. Here and there I would lay some money away. It wasn't much. Whatever extra dollars I could stash, I set aside into a secret fund that I kept in an old toolbox in the garage. Steadily, the cash added up and, on the night that I bid her farewell, I left with a little over four grand. I had figured that one day I might need it to pay support for a child I had forgotten or to square away an old debt. If such an event ever came to pass, I didn't want no help. I didn't want

Riley on the hook for my transgressions. I certainly didn't want her on the hook for this. Had I not squirreled that money away, I would have walked out with nothing. Kellen always had a knack for getting along while going without, anyway.

Be that as it may, having some spending money makes everything a hell of a lot easier. It allowed me to set my plans in motion quickly. I had no idea what kind of time I had to achieve my objectives. For all I knew, the clock had run out long ago, when my memories were still lost to blackness. It didn't matter. I had myself a starting point and that was good enough. If Bill, Wayne, and Polly weren't already in the ground, they were gonna be put there by my hand.

As it turned out, Bill was alive and as unwell as ever. No digging was required to track him down. Even as Paul Parker, Bill was known to me. A few years back, I went down a rabbit hole of internet articles. It was a slow night at work and I had nothing much else to do but sacrifice some idle time to the wifi. I read some third-rate expose that detailed the exploits of a cult leader that led a small and ragged band of his followers into the hills of Kentucky. I can't remember the particulars, but the name of his bizarre congregation, The Gatecrashers, had stuck with me. During my frantic weekend of remembrances and revenge fantasies, I set about looking for that article again.

Sure enough, he was still at it. His ministry even maintained a website that appeared to be sporadically updated. From the local newspaper online archives, I dug up old complaints that ordinary residents had made to the authorities against Bill's church. It seemed he had been accused of much the same malfeasance as so many other charlatan gurus before him. He violated zoning laws and led disenfranchised youths into his flock. He failed to pay his debts and plucked bored and previously regular citizens from their lives and led them into his unique brand of fervent insanity. None of that came as a concern to me. What mattered was that the most recent write-up on Bill was just four months old. That meant there was a good chance he was still up in them hills, preaching nonsense and poisoning impressionable minds. I tried to tell myself that I would be doing a public service by silencing Bill. But the fate and circumstances of others didn't much factor into my thinking. He was my target. If others found themselves freed due to his elimination, so be it. But I wasn't coming for them.

I employed Paul's steady hand to temper my rage and impatience. I may have had a destination, but I still required the means to get there. I knew that to do this right, I couldn't rush matters. I put my mind to more pressing concerns and set off toward territory occupied by miscreants and outlaws. It was now Kellen's hand that would be used.

I never saw it before, or not with any clarity, anyway. The dirt, the dilapidation, it was all there in Stone Horse. Yes, it is a charming little town, but it ain't perfect. I saw all that for the first time as I walked into town during the night. The asphalt of the streets was cracked and pockmarked. Some of the streetlights were burnt out and many residences and businesses alike held a certain degree of disrepair. Paul never saw such things. He could only see the beauty. That seems something of a foolish, perhaps a childish, way of looking at the world. Maybe so, but it's a wonderful way to live. But Paul's way of viewing the world amounted to nothing more than a passing curiosity. As it was, I was gonna have to venture further out to see my needs met. The town I had called home for two decades saw just a trickle from the rivers of poverty that weave their way through so much of the Midwest. Into those waters was where I had to go.

"You know who I am?" I asked to a kid who was pumping a few dollars' worth of fuel into his truck at the town's only gas station.

"No, sir," he replied softly, unsure of the true nature hiding behind my query.

"Seven dollars ain't going to take you far," I said as the pump clicked off.

"No, sir. But I don't have far to go," he said lightly, but with an underlying anxiety.

"I'll tell you what, you fill up your truck, and take another hundred for your troubles. I need a ride. You got the time?"

"Oh, it's after eleven, I think," he said.

"I wasn't asking the time, kid. I need a ride. You got time for that?" I asked sternly as I slapped a handful of twenties onto the hood.

"Look, mister, I don't want to get mixed up in anything."

"Now, there, we agree. I want a ride and I want you to have nothing to do with nothing else. I ain't up to anything illegal. You want some quick cash or not?" I asked, staring into him, impressing upon him that his only option was to agree.

"Sure, okay. But this is all on the square, right?"

"Kid, sooner or later, you're gonna learn that ain't nothing on the square, but what I'm asking of you is alright. Is that good enough for you?" I said, trying to soften my tone.

He nodded and I got in the truck. We pulled out and I directed him towards the Husker Manor Trailer Court. It was about an hour up the road, and its reputation was known to all in Stone Horse. I watched as the kid bristled, but he kept on driving without complaint.

"You ever been to Husker Manor?" I asked as starlight bled through the streaks on the windshield.

"No, sir."

"Good. Make this your first and last visit. Nothing good goes on up there," I said.

"Can I ask why you need to go there?"

"You can ask, but that don't mean I'm going to give you an answer. Put it this way, whatever happens after you drive away ain't gonna end up in the paper tomorrow."

I reached into my pocket and the kid damn near swerved off the road. I suppose he thought that I was reaching for a piece, but he steadied out once I held nothing more than my wallet.

"Here's an extra fifty," I began. "Outside of me giving you direction, I'm buying silence with my money. You got that? I say left, you nod and turn. I say right, you nod and turn. We understand each other?"

He nodded and I smiled. We kept on in silence, which suited me fine. I needed time to think. I imagine the lack of words put him off balance, but he kept to the task I had set before him. Finally, the trailer court came into view and I asked him to stop the truck.

"It's at least a mile or so up the road," he said.

"Yeah, well, be that as it may, this is as far as you go. I take it you're good with that?" I asked, to which he just chuckled shakily.

"Alright then," I said. "Take another hundred. Now, what I'm buying is your word. I know you're gonna tell your friends about this, that's just natural. But I want your word that you'll keep this transaction quiet for a week or so. Does that seem fair to you?"

"Yes, sir. My daddy always told me a man is only as good as his word," he said, trying, I suppose to say something that would please me.

"Your daddy sounds like a good man. But, truth be told, I really don't care. Take my money, keep your mouth shut, and forget my face. Oh, and kid, don't give rides to men like me again. You got lucky tonight. There's something else you need to know. There's only two kinds of men in this world, those that are for sale, and those that ain't. It's not easy, but try and be one of them that ain't," I said, hopping out of the truck.

He may have said something back to me, but I couldn't be bothered with none of that. Before I set three paces down the road, I heard that rickety diesel roar as the kid whipped it around in the middle of the road and sped away. I walked along the gravel, inspected the crooked welcome sign in the distance and my ears absorbed the tired hum given off from the bulbs of the lampposts overhead. I felt a kinship to the rough and unclean edges that surrounded me. I had a feeling that my good will would not extend to those I was to next meet.

I came into the trailer park. It looked to be the ruins of a city sacked decades before, left to rot with time. Most of the structures were abandoned. A few functioned as shelter for transients and as hideaways for the exploits of delinquent teens. As far as I knew, only three of the trailers housed permanent residents. These were the type of people that knew to mind their business and to keep their eyes away from the doings of others. They didn't peer out the windows to the sounds of argument or gunfire. They damn sure weren't the type to call on the law for assistance. However, there was only one among them that interested me, the infamous Trick Williams.

Trick kept himself scarce around Stone Horse but was known to all. He was the local boogeyman. He was rung up some years ago for fucking around with kids. Trick was said to cook up meth and loosely ran a prostitution ring of toothless hags and girls destined for death or prison before the age of thirty. He was also the kind of man who was known for his illicit wares. If a narcotic fix or untraceable gun was needed, Trick was the man to see. Furthermore, if there was something that had to get gone, Trick would see to that as well. It was in this trade of making items, both desirable and undesirable, appear and vanish that earned Trick his handle.

I stood before his trailer. The sides and skirt had been pulled away in random places, the roof bowed, and raw yellow light spilled out from the windows. I ascended the concrete blocks that served as steps to his front door, placed my boot against that barrier of thin wood and fiberglass, and kicked it from the hinges.

On a couch littered with cigarette burns and stains, sat Trick and a haggard girl. She was nearly naked and looked scared, although I couldn't suss out whether or not her fear sprung from the sight of me or if it was for the man seated beside her. While she was still and wide-eyed, Trick seemed barely conscious, but was full of movement. He tumbled from the couch, struggled to right himself, and shouted words both harsh and unintelligible.

I marched over, knocked the bottles and the ground-up

pills from the table, and ripped the girl from her seat. With one hand, I flung her toward the door. She tumbled down to be with the grime and debris upon the carpet, but quickly stood back up. With her spindly arms, she covered whatever exposed flesh that she could, and looked to me. I imagine that for so many years she had taken direction from men that to act of her own accord was a concept foreign to her. Perhaps impossible.

"Get the fuck out," I instructed, pointing to the doorway.

"I need my clothes," she voiced meekly.

"You need to go, I don't care where. Just don't come back here." And with that, she drifted out into the night.

"Hey, wake up," I said to Trick.

I seated myself on the couch. He was still wiggling about, wedged between the coffee table and where I sat. Trick was somewhat unaware of what was going on, so I tossed a plastic cup at his face. The contents of the cup splashed him in the eyes. I don't know what that liquid was, but it most have stung. I hoped it was piss. Whatever it may have been, it worked in gathering his attention.

"Who are you, man? Did Lenny send you? Hey, man, I told him before, I'm good for it. I just need some time. Ah, fuck, man, look at my fucking door!" he said, almost in tears, as he noticed the hole I had carved.

"I don't know no Lenny. I don't give a shit about him or your door. I need some things. I'm here to talk business, and I need you to pay attention," I said, resting my boot on Trick's chest.

"I don't know what you heard, but I'm just out here minding my own. Hey, look, if this is about that chick, she told me she was eighteen. Showed me ID and all," he said, still pleading in that squeaky voice of his.

"I don't care none for her either. I need a car, something reliable, and I need a gun. I got cash."

"Okay, yeah, alright, I might have some stuff laying around. But you're paying for my fucking door, man," said Trick, trying to sound forceful while still under another man's boot.

"I ain't paying for your door. A car, a gun, that's what I'm here for. What do ya got?"

"Can you at least relax, man?"

"Tell me you got something for me," I said coldly.

"I got this old Lumina out back. It's alright, the plate's clean," he said, and turned his face into an expression that begged for my satisfaction. Slowly, I lifted my leg, just enough to allow the worm to crawl out from beneath me.

"What about the gun? I just need a simple handgun, nothing fancy," I said.

"Yeah, man, I got you. I'm guessing you'd like ammo, too?" he asked, seemingly disgusted that I would also deprive him of a few bullets.

"Just enough to load it. Round the shit up. I'll give you a grand."

"Oh, no, man. No way. I can get fifteen hundred for the Lumina alone," he said, protesting much the same as a frightened child.

"This ain't no negotiation, Trick. We can both get something outta this, or I can take what I want. And that includes taking everything from you. I don't see no one else coming through that hole, offering you a thousand. It's your call," I said. I stared into him. I sincerely felt the desire to harm, to burn down his hovel and leave him lost under the smoldering remains. He saw such things in my eyes and, as he rose, Trick nodded in agreeance to my offer.

"Hey," I shouted as he made for outside. "Get the goddamn gun."

He seemed to sigh in discontentment before spinning around to make for the item I had demanded. I trailed closely behind as Trick staggered about, making his way into his decrepit bathroom. He dug around under the sink, tossing assorted bottles and random tools out of the way. Before he could rise, I swooped down and wrenched the revolver from his hand. I stood above him for a moment with that heavy lump of metal in my hand. I paused long enough for him to feel a cloud of abject vulnerability settle over his position.

"Bullets," I said. I turned away and made for the yard.

Trick wandered out to meet me. He slapped some rounds into my hand and then directed me over to the Lumina. It sat under the droop of a crooked tree and weeds had grown tall enough to lick at the side mirrors with the persuasion of the wind.

"Start it," I said while digging into my pocket for my bundle of twenty-dollar bills.

He did as he was told and so did that old Lumina. I didn't react right off. I stood there, in the dark, among exhaust fumes and the distant glow of cheap, artificial light. I studied him, how he twitched, how his eyes refused to meet mine. This all felt too familiar to me. The scene of decay around us, the actors in this play, themselves decayed things. Whether or not I liked it, I had returned to my natural habitat, and I was ready to go hunting.

"So, man, you got that grand, right?" he asked. I didn't answer as I peeled off the promised amount. I kept my gaze locked onto him and, in silence, transferred the money. Quietly, I settled into the car and drove off.

In that moment of leaving, I felt outside myself. I was calm, disquietingly calm, if there can be such a condition. It was as though I observed this event through the eyes of a far-away stranger. I had a sense of gliding into the car like a ghost and, once I put it in gear, I imagined the sight of my new automobile vanishing like an iron phantom into the fog. I learned that there was no more hope of redemption. Everything I had known had been divided and placed into one of two piles, *before this* or *after this*.

17. Eastbound And All The Way Down

I drove into the night until I crossed out of Nebraska. I needed rest and the cheap motel that greeted my arrival in

Missouri felt an ideal place to crash. I fell into sleep quickly. I was untroubled by thoughts of being found or otherwise disturbed. Trick and his neighbors weren't the type to bring their grievances to the cops. He sure as hell weren't gonna involve the law in none of his affairs. Besides, I knew the thousand I had given him was enough to put the events of one unfortunate evening far from his mind. I figured that at some point, Riley was going to file a missing persons report. But what did that matter? It would be days before her pleas were taken seriously and there was nothing nobody could do. I, a grown man, left of my own accord. As far as the law would see it, I was gone but not missing. That would have to wait until later.

Before the rising of the sun, I took back to the road. Those first seven hours of my travels went by as though blinked away. My mind kept spinning back to thoughts of Riley and the kids. The remembrances of them were welcome and sweet. I was savoring the memories of a life I left behind. It was a life now done, but I felt fortunate all the same. It didn't last, but the fact that it had happened at all warmed me. It was a life I would never again know, and I made my peace with all that. It was those left behind, the family I had left among the wreckage, that poisoned my thoughts. Threads of guilt were weaving their way into me. Shame wouldn't be far behind.

I exited the highway and settled down into the least crowded area of a roadside diner. I ordered a meal that is now lost to memory and used the time to focus my attention on Bill. he and his flock had settled among the rolling hills and dense growth of the woods between Owensboro and Elizabethtown, Kentucky. I knew that by the black of night I would find myself in the Bluegrass State. My thinking then went to the rising of the sun. I wondered if it was the type of thing that Bill paused to admire and appreciate. I had my doubts about that and I sincerely hoped that he would sleep through sunrise. I wanted him to miss it so that when the end came for him, he would be made to reflect upon all the events, trivial and magnificent alike, that he had taken for granted and would never again experience.

I had finished my meal and was set to depart. My time in the diner was quiet and uneventful, but before I could take back to the road, a little flicker of excited tension came to call. I was alone in a booth, plates of scattered scraps and an empty glass before me. Without any words of introduction, a young woman slid into the seat on the other side of the table. I wasn't startled, but I must have appeared caught off guard, as she quickly apologized for the intrusion.

"Sorry. If you could spare some time, do you mind if I ask you a few questions? This won't take long, promise," she said in the perky but nervous cadence of someone who found themselves a legal adult but still shackled to all the uncertainty of adolescence.

I bristled and said nothing. My mind went to thoughts of the law even though the only crime I had so far committed was kicking in Trick's front door. She hadn't come to see me about such things and she damn sure weren't no cop. I didn't recognize her and I thought her too young to know Riley. Besides, Riles wasn't the type to send others out to do her work. If she had a mind to tail me, she would have done so herself and found me much sooner. I couldn't figure this girl. My mind then went to darker places. She came to me as an obstacle, and I entertained all the ways of going about ridding myself of her presence.

"Um," she began. "My name's Allison. I'm a writer. Well, I want to be, anyway. So, I, uh, collect stories. I like to do short interviews with people and kinda compile everything. I'm working on a collection that I want to put together in a book about conversations with random strangers. Sounds sorta dumb, huh? Well, I noticed you over here by yourself and thought you looked interesting. Mysterious, maybe? I don't know."

"Mysterious." I said this slowly and with a smile that made her visibly uneasy. She was young, but old enough to differentiate a common smile from a pleasant-looking mask employed to hide all manner of ugliness and ill intention.

"Yeah, I guess," she said softly, brushing back from her eyes a handful of tight brown curls.

"So, you want me to tell you a story?" I asked, but made it sound more like a challenge.

"Sure, yeah, fire away. I have some questions I like to ask, but sometimes the best stuff is just raw. The stuff that just comes natural, you know?"

She had more to say, or maybe she just had more broken phrases to trip over. Either way, I shushed her by bringing a finger up to my lips. I gave her the same stare that I had inflicted on Trick and started talking.

"A long time ago, another girl thought I was mysterious. She took me in and I lived with her for years, decades, really. Her kids became my kids. Our lives became *our life*. But I'll tell you something about mysteries, Allison, you ain't never ready when the truth decides to surface. I left her not two days back. When I stepped out into the night she was nothing but a pile of tears and broken feelings on a couch. And right now, I ain't of the mind to feel the least bit bad about it," I said, keeping my gaze upon her.

She sighed and words tried to crackle their way from her throat, but nothing of consequence came out. She leaned back in the booth, not to relax, but to increase the distance between herself and me.

"You're trying to find the polite way around this," I said. "There's only so much time we all got. You'll come to find that there exist circumstances that leave no time for being polite. Ask your questions and get on with it, or move on from it, whatever that happens to be at the time. I'll make this easy on you. You get one for free. You wanna know the reason why I left, don't you?" I asked, to which she just nodded.

"I'm fixing on killing some people, if they're still even alive. I'm hoping to put three in the ground. Any more than that would be cruel, unjust. But I will not shy from my objective. By any means necessary, Allison. That's how the difficult things get done."

"I, I have to leave," she said and hurriedly grabbed her belongings. In her haste, she spilled her purse. "Shit, oh shit," she said, frantically, and with enough volume to attract attention. As she scrambled to jam the contents back into her bag, I eased back in my seat and picked at the leftover scraps on my plate.

"Hey, Allison," I called to her just as she rose. "Good luck with your book."

Once back on the highway, I gave some time to considering my conversation with Allison. I took some enjoyment in giving her a start, but I couldn't work out no higher reason for what I had done. It was just something to do to kill time before it came time for killing. That was the problem, I was impatient. I had hours left to travel and I wanted it all over with. The minutes that followed were long and nettlesome. The hours were worse. All the way to Kentucky, I gave not one thought to Riley, or the kids, or Nebraska in general. Hell, I didn't even think much about Wayne or Polly. I stayed focused on Bill. I didn't wonder about what to say to him or how I might go about seeing to his murder. I simply thought about it being a bothersome chore that needed done.

The light was leaving the sky by the time I had crossed into Kentucky and navigated my way into the county that housed Bill's congregation of misfits and throwaways. I rode slowly through small towns and villages, each seemingly swept clean of activity by the rise of the moon. Occasionally I would spot someone walking a lonely road, or a cluster of folks congregated on a porch or outside a corner bar. They all had the same look in their eyes. It was one of suspicion that carries with it the promise of danger. I had come, in the night, from the outside. These folks who studied me as I cruised past were not stupid. They were not yokels, paranoid of those that came from parts unknown. They were familiar with unsavory men and could detect such creatures with all the clarity of a bloodhound. In a strange way, I felt a connection to those whose eyes I had only met in passing glances. We knew each other. We had an understanding. They would do me the courtesy of minding their business so as long as I was of the mind to mind mine.

I knew my route to Bill could have been made easier by inquiring about him to the locals, but this was a fool's option. Complications would come attached to my queries and loose ends would trail behind me. I was on my own.

My Lumina rattled on past junk shops cleverly disguised as antique stores. I observed structures that looked long-since abandoned, but knew too well that they still functioned as residences. Shuttered factories were given over to the growth of weeds and the decay that time brings. Storefronts were boarded up and the seesaws and swing sets of old playgrounds were rusted through and partially dismantled. I was among the poor and forgotten things. I could feel Bill everywhere, though I knew he was smart enough to hide a bit further off. He needed to go beyond the dilapidation and press deeper into the wilderness that lies beyond civilization.

During my journey through a small town that looked much the same as others put in my rearview, I parked the car and got out. I wandered an empty road under the flickering glow given off from a crooked streetlamp. I peered into a secondhand store. A cloak of dust hung over the items. Old magazines, figurines of saints and angels, cheap toys, and all manner of articles emblazoned with the image of Confederate flags shared space in the front window display. My eyes drifted across the discards of others until they stopped and fixed themselves onto a pair of slave shackles. They seemed to have been placed there as an afterthought. They were tucked in a corner and a handwritten price tag revealed their value of ninety dollars. I was not an easy man to shake, but I felt disturbed by what was seen. This item, if indeed they were authentic, once carried free men into a life of slavery and torment. They were the symbol of families, generations, broken. And there they sat, displayed as whimsical trinkets.

I turned back to my car but paused to observe a person that

had taken to observing me. Through the low light, I watched as the figure stood still. It was partially obscured by shadows near the end of the road. I could not make out the gender or any other defining details from such a distance. The only sign of life given from my audience was in the way it rhythmically brought a cigarette up to its lips and then allowed the arm to drop again with each exhalation of smoke. I made not a motion and my counterpart appeared unfazed by my stare. I stood there long enough for this specter to finish its cigarette, flick the butt to the ground, and slowly drift off into the shadows of an alley. I grinned in the dark and got back in the car.

18. Gatecrasher

Putting distraction from my mind, I refocused on my task. Using the information I had gained from the complaint reports about Bill, I set a course into the wilderness. I wound through the hills upon unlit roads that devolved into ever-narrowing dirt pathways. Along my travels I passed proper signs that were put up to ward off trespassers, and I viewed warnings of hand-painted cardboard that had been nailed to trees. The signs felt to me much the same as the rotted archways that loom over deserted concentration camps. They were things once horrible that had since gone impotent.

The night was perfectly dark and all encompassing. It felt plausible that I would come to find alien life in those woods well before I would come to find another human being. If Bill had indeed carved out a burrow in those hills, he had done a fine job of hiding himself away. In a few hours, day would break, and I was growing tired. I was beginning to lose heart when, at once, a glimmer came through the trees. I felt my blood thunder with excitement as I studied the glow. It twinkled at me through the forest like starlight. The many points of light I saw took turns flickering. They would fade into the darkness and then reappear in sequence. This rhythm told a story of its own. It told of a source of light in the background, its glow regularly interrupted by objects passing before it. My mind took to fantasies of witches dancing around fires. This seemed as possible a place as any for the cult leader I sought. I nudged my car off the path and into the weeds. I got out and walked toward the light.

It was as though I was being pulled into the woods, over bitter earth, among the cacophonous whirl of insect chatter. My pace was slow, as the darkness conspired with every rise of root and undulation of the ground to impede my advance. None of that mattered. Soon enough, music found my ears and, even with my vision impaired, I could follow the sound to its source. If I were indeed to come upon Bill, the music betrayed what is usually thought of when one considers a cult leaders' choice for aural ambiance.

I might have had no expectations at all for such things, but if I put some thought to it, something psychedelic, trippy and sunny, would have been what I imagined was played for the faithful. Maybe, during my time as Paul, I had watched too much TV and forgotten who I was dealing with. Bill did things, all things, just a tick off from normal. It should have come as no surprise then that his cult, even down to the small details, would be altogether different from other brands of religious zealotry.

As I drew close enough to make out the shapes and shadows as those cast by human beings, the nature of the music being played became clear. It was one piece of music, relatively short, but looped over and over again. It was a minimalist composition built from a backbone of a few low notes that seemed to reverberate out into the forest and to the cosmos beyond. Rhythmic bass swells came and went, accompanied only by the howl of a single voice. It was barely audible and seemed to have been recorded far from the microphone that was responsible for picking up its haunting call. I got to thinking that the voice I was hearing was Bill's. It was like he was saying hello through a dense filter of madness. I was of the mind to answer back.

I arrived in a clearing, mere paces from folks scattered about. Some lay asleep in the dirt, others were down on their knees, swaying and moaning along with the music. A few people walked around aimlessly. More still simply stood in place and stared at the sky and its endless well of stars. I took note of two curiosities. The first was that no one was dressed alike. There wasn't even a uniformity to their states of coverage. This lack of outward cohesion I found odd. Again, this was no ordinary cult, if such things can be ordinary. The second observation I made was that not a soul spoke to me or even seemed to register my presence there among them. In a way, I knew they saw me. It just so happened that no one cared.

I looked about the encampment, which it was more so than a proper compound. Shabby lean-tos had been built. Old RVs and passenger cars appeared to function as residences, as did rotted out pop-up trailers. Common tents littered the ground. Behind the music, the hum of a generator could be heard. It no doubt powered the stereo and the colored Christmas lights that were strung through the trees and attached to the tents and other structures. What I viewed put a sickness in my gut. I had laid eyes on something like this before, something equally mad, but this was much more perverse. I thought of my time spent in Xalbadora's old room and the day it took me to uncover her writings. This was much the same. I was standing again inside the mind of another. This time, however, all the noise, confusion, and tangled wiring was exposed. Bill wasn't just somewhere in amongst all the disorder, he was the disorder.

"Why you here?" A woman of middle age asked me this. She appeared distant from reality, barely tethered to the ground, but I sensed she was not high. Her eyes darted about but never to me. She put a hand out between us, like she was about to press her palm against my chest, but she never touched more than air.

"I'm looking for someone," was all I said.

"You found him," she said with a smile, eyes wet with tears. With that, she backed away from me, into the darkness between the trees.

I watched her as she disappeared. I then considered the idea that she may never return. My trivial pondering was broken once a small strobe light began to flash from the inside of an old shipping container. With that incessant flickering, the dozen or so people that surrounded me, even those previously fast asleep, all rose and walked calmly, but with purpose, to the open doors of the container. I made no movement. I elected to observe them as they filed in, and then stood alone for a moment. I felt the cool morning air around me. Among the prism of colored lights that fell over me and the eerie song that continued to mingle with the dark of the forest, I stared into the open end of the container. In between bright white flashes, blackness spilled forth from it, almost like I could watch the dark roll out like thick liquid as it gurgles from a bottle tipped over. Sometimes in life, there are truths known before they can be stated as fact. One such truth was that Bill was inside that container and he was the reason for the gathering. I followed behind the flock, the wolf among the sheep.

I crossed into the container but paused there on its threshold. The corrugated steel walls were decorated by tinsel, stands of disused lights, and artwork that I recognized as laid down by Bill's hand. Oddly, his skill set seemed to have dulled with time, as no aspect of these paintings rose to the talent level of the mural he had painted all those years ago for Wayne, Polly, and myself. The scenes were biblical in nature but warped all the same. I don't know the Good Book well, but there were inconsistencies and contradictions in the images that Bill created. Alien-looking creatures took charge of the crucifixion of Christ. Viking longboats sailed over, and were crumbled by, the parting of the Red Sea, and Moses was rendered female. She came down from a mountain with tablets in her hands, but the commandments thereupon were not etched over common stone. For reasons unknown, Bill had chosen to swap out rock in favor of bloody human torsos. The words of God were carved into the backs but, though still legible, each commandment had been scratched out. To Bill, his god had fucked up, and through this work of art, Bill saw to it that corrections were made.

I took a seat in a metal folding chair at the rear of the container. Before me were another two dozen like chairs, but only half were occupied. I had no way of knowing if Bill's followers had shrunk in number over time or if these seats always remained empty. During the pulses of strobe light, I took to studying the members of the congregation. There didn't appear a common thread to bind together this motley collection of parishioners. Most were somewhere between young adulthood and middle age, but there were the exceptions. Three members of the church were elderly. There was also a child, perhaps no older than ten. She was every bit as dead-eyed and oblivious to the world outside the woods as those around her. Curiously, no one there struck me as being her primary caregiver. I would have laid good money on the bet that neither of her biological parents were in attendance.

It might seem reasonable that anxiety would have gripped me in that moment, but I felt calm. I was truly still of body and mind. I was patient. The first act of my plan was nothing more than a formality then. In some way, with my restraint, I imagine I was savoring the moment. I allowed my eyes to linger on the altar. It was constructed of bowed plywood, overlaid with a ragged tablecloth. Faded images of flowers were screened into the cloth and they were runover by streaks of old stains. I wanted to see Bill take his place behind the altar. I was curious to see how the years had changed him. I longed to hear him preach.

Like a snake as it wriggles from under the cover of fallen leaves, Bill floated out from behind a curtain and stood behind the altar. There came no cheers, no applause. Everyone simply turned their gazes to him, grew still and quieter than before. Through the flickering of the light, this rapid fluctuation between intense bright and conquering black, I saw Bill in jerky frames. He remained as I remembered, thin, gaunt, and of an ill pallor. However, he was not the same man I once knew. His clothes appeared clean and selected with purpose. His hair had thinned but it was freshly cut and styled back tight, like the wing of a bird at rest. A part of me anticipated hearing his sermon would be a comical affair. I felt sinister as I welcomed such levity before acting on my murderous intentions. What came to my ears, though, was wholly unexpected. The uncertainty, the nervousness that once strangled his speech, was gone. In madness, Bill had found an area in which to excel.

"God! God doesn't love you!" he boomed. "If I know His mind, and I know His mind, I say that God hates us all."

Bill paused for a while and let the sentiment hang in the air. He left his arms outstretched and looked to the metal ceiling above. His expression was full of pleas. It was like he was trying to commune directly with the divine. Bill behaved as though he alone knew the truth and was trying his best to impart such wisdom to his wretched and ignorant audience. Bill was asking his master for patience.

"And who among you could blame Him?" he continued. "He doesn't want your prayers. He doesn't want your worship. He doesn't even want to know your name! We are but an experiment that has failed the creator for thousands of years. Every day more are born to His service only to do nothing with such favor. We toil and die, and we fail. None have seen His kingdom and none ever will until we secure it. Not with prayer! Not with worship! But with action!" he screamed, before continuing in a whisper. "You can only secure a place by His side with sacrifice. *Your* sacrifice. It is in death that He will see how worthy we are."

He sounded triumphant and tears filled his eyes. In that moment, I knew not what he was getting at, but I considered myself lucky to have arrived when I did. It seemed clear that the endgame for his church was close to being realized, and the time to see Bill put in the ground by my hand was running out. This notion set my mind into a problematic way of thinking. If, indeed, he was fixing on dying any time soon, how could I properly punish him for the transgressions he once committed against me? Just then, more than anything, I felt annoyed, and my impatience surfaced. But with it came the desire to learn more about the man who lead a flock he had dubbed The Gatecrashers. I steadied myself, determined to hear him through.

"Failure," he began again, in an exasperated voice. "Failures are we all. But it doesn't have to be this way. Not anymore. Like the child that wastes his food today because more will be served tomorrow, we have wasted the opportunity that God has so selflessly given. That opportunity is in His service. To sound the horns of His glory. To be the continuation of His shadow that will come to smother all those without belief. To etch His name into the face of eternity. And, to take our place, finally, at His side. We will not call to Him. We will not pray to Him. We will worship Him, not with an empty chorus of meaningless voices. No, we will not insult Him with our cheap praise. We will fight for Him. We will take the battle to His enemies."

As Bill went about repeating himself, I folded my arms across my chest and looked to those around me. I would say that no one seemed enraptured by what was preached. I'm not for certain any of them were all that interested. But that's when it all got to me. Bill was warning against getting stuck in the mire of endless chatter. They were done talking and they were done listening. He had succeeded in beating indecision from them. It was the time for action and he saw it in their vacant expressions. His followers weren't so hollowed out after all. They were bored. It must have registered with him that they were ready to take the next step. Finally, Bill's preaching lead to a point and he laid out his challenge.

"Satan. It has always been Satan," said Bill with calm authority. "He is a collector of failures and, I know, just as disappointed as God in our interminable malaise. We've done wrong by Satan just as we have done wrong by God. The time has arrived to end all that. He is the mightiest of enemies, and he deserves battle. But not just any battle. He deserves to know pain at the hands of God's most faithful servants. We are those servants. We are the ones chosen by our Lord to deliver His message to Satan. Imagine how He would look upon us were we to bring one so lost as Satan back to the flock. This is our fate. To crash the gates of Hell and wring its wayward master from the fire. This action will require all your courage, all your resolve, and all of our deaths. We will seek no absolution. We will go willingly to our graves as sinners. As our souls rocket toward the gates of Hell, we will welcome the vision, and we will not shy before the Morning Star. Together, we will return him to God's endless sky."

I guess it's natural to want to riddle out madness. Maybe that would make it appear less horrible. I can't say, but I was guilty of trying to work my way into Bill's manner of thinking. His proposition was to lead a ragged pack of misfits into the depths of Hell, and there, by whatever means, his goal was to usurp Satan. I never put no stock in religious teaching, but supposing God and all the rest are real, I couldn't figure how Bill saw his small group as an army up to the task. I would probably have gone on putting my mind further to this subject, but my attention was snapped back to the moment when at once the strobe light stopped. For a few minutes the container was filled with blackness. I heard the scraping of chairs and the rustling of clothes. I felt a breeze created by the movement of the people as they filed past me and back out into the coming of dawn. I remained and, as a lone bulb of a table lamp sparked to life, I saw Bill seated before me.

"Hello, brother Kellen. I have longed for such a day," said Bill with a warm smile.

I was without words. Through the haze and the disorientation brought about by the strobe light, he had recognized me. He didn't seem alarmed by my presence, or even surprised. He was pleased to see me, and I felt he had not one worry as to my intentions. To Bill, everything that had happened between us and in the years that followed was more proof of God's plan.

"I always felt we would meet again," he said as I stayed quiet. "You were always too much of a force to go unnoticed by our Lord. He has sent you here to lead us in our objective. I have taken the people as far as I can in this life. After our deaths, I will gladly put my flock in your hands."

"And after all this dying, are you coming along, or are you staying behind?" I asked.

"Kellen, I am committed to God," he said incredulously. "At the end, and into the evermore, I will go right at your side and at the side of the others."

"So, suicide, then?" I asked.

"Suicide is an affront to Him. It will guarantee us passage to Satan."

"Alright, fair enough. When you figure this should happen?"

"The moment that I saw you walk into my church, I knew God was telling me it was time. The morning He has sent us is beautiful. I speak of action, Kellen. Let today be the day we truly serve God," said Bill, wholly comfortable with his decision. "I will inform the others that the hour of our great trial is nigh."

"Let today be the day," I echoed. "Let today be the day. In the past, we might not have agreed on much, but we agree on this. Only thing is, though, you're going alone."

Before I had properly finished speaking, I tore a strand of Christmas lights from the wall and set upon Bill. His thin frame collapsed under me and he offered only meek resistance as I coiled the thin wires around his neck. I pulled the slack tight and held him against the dirty floor with my knees. I knew not how long it would take to strangle someone to death, but it felt to me a considerable amount of time went by before I allowed my grip to loosen.

As the first rays of daylight bled into the container, I looked to Bill. The lifelessness in his eyes was unmistakable. I didn't bother to check for a pulse or put my hand in front of his mouth to feel for breath. He was dead. I felt no emotion as I looked at him. He didn't even look like a creature who, just minutes before, was alive. He appeared to my eyes like a piece of furniture discarded in a corner. I don't remember sweating or feeling labored. I felt no sense of accomplishment, relief, or shame. He was as I expected, a chore that got done and merited nothing more than to be moved on from. Quietly, I stepped away and exited the container.

The fresh daylight burned my eyes and the scent of rank weeds and unwashed bodies filled my nose. I looked about the encampment. Under the glare of the sun, it revealed itself more unappealing than before. This place that Bill's followers had made their home resembled an old refugee hideaway for those seeking escape from the tyranny of third-world warlords. An air of sickness and despair swam about those woods. I found in myself no sympathy for those that had willingly followed Bill into the wilderness, but then I remembered that little girl.

To find her would add complications to my task. If I could locate her, I could take her to safety. However, I might have to do so by force. This could lead to all manner of unwanted attention and, at the very least, delay my progress. I thought little of being identified. Given the mental states of the adults I had observed, they likely would have difficulty describing themselves. Children can be rather different. They have a clarity about them that often gets overlooked. I wanted to leave, to abandon her to the beasts. This was once done to me and the ultimate result has proved disastrous. Even so, I felt no obligation to cast myself as her keeper. I didn't, but Paul did.

Unable to quiet the ghost I carried, I set off in search of her. I peeled back tent flaps only to find empty beds made of torn sheets and newspaper. On occasion, I came across one of the flock in sleep. Even at rest, they seemed unbalanced, not human, but more like a rabid animal as it shivers at the coming of death. Not many of the vehicles I checked were occupied. Most weren't even locked, but the ones that were bothered me little and proved to be no deterrent. I kicked in the doors of the

RVs and smashed car windows to uncover the identities of those squirreled away under blankets. Those that were awake and those that I disturbed stared and studied me. I was something of a curiosity, but no one spoke to me or offered resistance. I came to suspect that behavior such as mine wasn't uncommon in the camp.

The girl was not to be found. I tried to tell myself, or Paul, specifically, that she wasn't actually a child. Perhaps she was just a small and malnourished woman. I entertained the idea that she never existed at all. It wasn't beyond reason to suggest that my mind invented her among all the confusion that I had previously immersed myself in. I couldn't rightly convince Paul of this, so I kept on searchin'.

I trailed off into the woods and came upon a woman. I do not know with any certainty if she was the same woman I had spoken to earlier. She was naked but for a heavy collection of dirt that had stuck to her skin. Her hair was wound into knots, and she made no attempt to cover herself after she noticed my approach. I walked to within spitting distance of her and tried to find some measure of lucidity in her gaze. I could detect nothing of the sort, but after a few moments of study she spoke to me.

"You were the one who had a private audience with brother William? You are truly blessed," she said slowly.

"There was a girl in that container. You seen her?" I asked.

"I have seen the truth and glory of our Lord, thanks to brother William."

"The girl. I need to find her. It's important," I insisted.

"She likes to sleep atop the church. To be closer to God," the woman said with a wide smile. She was beaming with pride as she looked up to the sky and began to weep. "Please, will you tell me what he said?" she asked, her face still tilted to the clouds.

"He said he was wrong," I said, and stepped away.

I left her alone to deal with the whims of insanity as I followed a path back to the camp. No more activity had sprung up, but as I inspected the container, Bill's oversized coffin, as it were, I spotted a flow of thin, blonde hair as it had spilled down the side of the structure. I upended a pallet that had been used as a table, splattering its contents onto the ground. I propped it against the side of the container and climbed up. The child seemed suspended somewhere between proper sleep and the exhaustion that forces the sick into listlessness. I flung her spindly body over my shoulder and made for the ground.

I left the camp, and not a soul questioned me over my intentions with the girl. This angered me further as she lay folded and motionless in my arms. I carried her through the woods and thought that my journey would end in that forest. If someone of sound mind would have spotted me, all that I had set out to accomplish would have been undone. I felt foolish and thought to discard the girl. I could not do such a thing. Paul's influence was too strong. Maybe he was trying to stop me. Maybe he would continue to try and sabotage me every step of the way. This was a variable I hadn't considered. Indecision would unman me, so I resolved to see this episode through, but I also vowed to steel myself against Paul moving forward.

In the car and back on the road, the girl remained asleep. She was curled up on the passenger seat. Dirt and leaf litter dropped from the bottoms of her feet and from her clothes with every jostle of the car. As I looked at her, I thought of demons. Not in any biblical sense, but in the ways that they're talked about by the mentally ill. Such creatures trail behind us all in legions, foaming at the mouth and screaming. We try and shed 'em the best we can, or bury deep the ones that we can't shake loose. I had more than my fair share, and maybe I got caught up in trying to peel one off by helping that girl. I don't know, but I did come to realize something. Nothing I did that day was gonna spare that child her devils.

I drove slowly out of the hills and wound my way back toward civilization. The girl stirred on occasion but didn't fully wake. I scanned my surroundings for a suitable location on which to unload my burden. I figured on a church being the best move. I thought it cruel to expose that poor child to more religion, however, my reasoning served not her purposes but mine. I was counting on those attending mass to first comfort and care for the girl before they tilted their attention to the *wheres* and *whys* of her deliverance from The Gatecrashers. I pulled over and parked a couple of blocks down from the church. I was ready to set the girl upon the curb and speed away, but before I could take such action, I noticed her eyes as they studied me.

"Don't look at me, look that way," I said, as I pointed straight ahead. She complied and I went on talking before she could give voice to nosy questions. "You know what's back there?" I asked, gesturing to the rear window.

"The backseat?" she asked quietly, staring straight ahead.

"No. That back there behind us is all that's over and done with, that's how it's gonna stay, and there ain't no undoing any of it. Over here, where I'm sitting, you got no reason to look. That's because I'm right next to you. We're in the same damn spot. Just to look to either side of you is a lateral move. It don't make no sense and it'll get you nowhere but stuck. That," I said, drawing attention to the world outside the windshield. "That is where you want to look. It's the only move we all got. Go forward or you go fucking nowhere. You understand what I'm telling you, girl?"

"I think so."

"That's good enough for now. At least you're thinking about what I said. Think on it some more. Someday you'll get it. Hey, one more thing. Now, don't look at me, but tell me what I look like," I said.

"I don't know," said the girl.

"Sure you do. Think about that, describe me."

"Umm, you're old," she said, with all the innocent honesty of a child.

I didn't reply right off. What she had said made me smile. This was the first time since my memories returned that I think

I smiled a genuine expression of happiness. I knew it was Paul that was smiling, but I let myself enjoy it all the same. I suppose that's because I wanted this go-round of being Kellen Black to be different. I would need small moments of levity such as this to keep me in line. To accomplish what I had tasked myself with required clarity. But, also, I needed little joys, those savored by the ordinary person, to remind me that Polly, Wayne, Bill and myself were far removed from common and decent man.

"That's right, and you don't need to think of me no other way. Now, I want you to get out of the car and walk into that church over there," I said.

"Why?"

"Because that's what's ahead of you."

"Where will you go?" she asked.

"In the other direction."

19. Legacy Of Savagery

The overwhelming need to escape, to flee, impressed itself upon me. I can't figure why. My mind didn't wander to logical thinking that involved complications and consequences. Instead, I felt something like fear. I was afraid, but I didn't know why. I had this sensation that gnawed at me and, no matter how strong the bite, I couldn't place the source of my torment.

Once that little girl had made her way to the steps of the church, I turned the car around and drove away. I kept on, stopping for nothing, until I crossed over into Ohio. I didn't consider whether or not this made logical sense for my undertaking. I just needed to cross a line that clearly marked off one thing from another. It was like I had to reset, not just for the tasks ahead, but I had to adjust my overall thinking.

I stopped for gas and filled up, but I didn't get back in the car right away. I was alone at a gas station that sat among wide swaths of empty countryside. I walked a few paces toward the road with the breeze around me and the sun on my back. I allowed myself some time to process the events from the morning. I got to thinking that my act of goodwill with the child is what served to unsettle me. The move I had made was not in Kellen's playbook. To just see it all through, taking it upon myself to shelter that girl, felt much the same as having a foreign and malignant fluid injected into the blood.

I wrestled with the notion of calling the whole thing off, giving in, and calling it quits. The concept of revenge seemed rather hollow in that moment. If I could achieve my goals, what difference would it make in the grand scheme? I had to give that question some consideration, and I also had to acknowledge the fact that Kellen, as he once was, was gone. I think I wanted him back too badly. It would have made everything simpler, but ain't nothing about life and the living of it that's simple.

I came to realize that, for the first time in my life, I knew who I was. I wasn't Kellen and I wasn't Paul. They weren't characters that starred in separate acts of the same play, Kellen and Paul were two halves that had been hastily stitched together to form one man. I was the mixture of them both. Sometimes the oil rose to the surface, and at other times, clear water is all that showed, but both elements were always there. This kind of epiphany should be an event that settles the mind. For most people, I imagine that's true. For me, though, it came like a devastation. This reality told me that during my youth, I always had it in me to go right and do good, I just couldn't be bothered. It also illuminated the fact that I was capable of all manner of evil when I lived with Riley and the kids. I felt dirty, like I went about exposing good folks to some infection that I carried.

I settled back into the car and put it in gear. Taking a last look into the rearview mirror, I knew the only way left for me to go was forward. It may not have been the right or virtuous path to take, but it was the path that I had managed to cut and shape with the choices I had made. I thought of destiny and what an absurd concept that is. Destiny don't exist. It's just a fancy word that gets tossed around when there ain't no options left.

The car might have been full of fuel, but I sure as hell weren't. I cruised on until I spied a fast food restaurant. I swung into the drive-thru and didn't cast a thought as to what I might order. Sitting in line behind four or five others, I peered through the windows of the restaurant and studied those seated inside. Initially, there was no real point to this exercise, I was just killing time. Soon enough, though, my observation bent itself into morbid fascination.

I noticed a couple. They were seated across from each other at a booth. I figured both to be in their 60s, but the telltale signs of hard livin' were branded onto their faces. Their bodies seemed racked with discomfort, and their postures told of the costs paid to past sicknesses. I didn't notice them say anything to one another, and it appeared that they took turns looking down at their food and then gazing wearily off into the distance. If I had studied them for an hour, I doubt that their eyes would have ever met. I was sure that neither wanted to be where they had found themselves, but this was the end result of the choices they each had made.

I surmised that, in their youths, each had run off whatever better options there might have been. They seemed the type to steal and cheat, and to have arrogance enough to feel that they could cheat the clock. Time is a persistent force, though. It's always gonna win. By catching up or running out, it's gonna win. And there before me, behind grease-stained glass, sat two miserable creatures afflicted by the indifferent whims of time. They were broke, broken, and defeated, the pained ghosts of the unscrupulous people they once were. This sad vision came to me like a mirror. I felt like I knew them, and then, I thought of the parents I had never known.

Although I can't say if the story of me coming into the world inside an old gas station holds any truth, it's the story I know and it seems plausible enough. Furthermore, I don't really know what state I was born in, but Ohio is the safe bet.

Maybe in some weird, unconscious way, that is why I drove there that day. However it may have started for me, I thought the couple that I viewed to be just the type to dump an infant. Those types tend not to stay together, if they even properly knew one another to begin with, and those kinds of people usually don't have longevity of their side. Pushing all that into the corners for the time, I think I went about fantasizing about that couple being my family. There they were, poor and exhausted, languishing through the last miserable years of their lives. And there I was, their son, the product of their wretchedness, equally discontent and maladjusted, stopping for a cheap bite before carrying on with their legacy of savagery. We would pass each other on by and never be the wiser.

I then sunk under the waves of some especially sorrowful thought. I knew of no blood family, but I had them all the same. Creatures like me, as surprising as it may seem, do not just rise out of the dark earth or surface from the depths of swamps. We are born of ordinary human beings, much the same as scientists, presidents, and professors. That reality meant that there was a mathematical chance that I had, in fact, known members of my family at one time or another, yet never knew who they were. I had cousins, aunts, uncles, siblings, possibly. Did I ever assault, steal from, or beat any of them? Some junkie-trash girl I had raped in an alley in my teens could have been my sister. In the most perverse of universes, this would almost seem fair, to have the beasts cannibalize each other.

I turned my thoughts to the family I did know, not Riley and the kids, but Polly and the old gang. They deserved to be done in, I still clung to that, but the deed needed to be an inside job, so to speak. It was fitting, karmic justice. I had been written into a Greek tragedy and I was obligated to play out my role.

A car horn alerted my distracted mind to the impatience of the driver behind me and shook me out of the darkness that had snapped its jaws shut around my thoughts. I felt no anger in that moment. I was in the wrong as I tarried in the queue. I pulled up, placed my order, and took the sharp noise of that horn as an act of mercy.

20. Bitter Harvest

Early the next day, I set out in search of a local library. I eased myself in front of one of the computers and set my mind back to the task of tracking down Wayne and Polly. It seemed that in the years that had followed my disposal at their hands, they had all gone to ground. I never entertained the notion that they had cleaned themselves up and gone right. Reason suggested that after I was quite literally tossed aside, they all laid low. I imagine the boredom this created was nigh unbearable, especially for Polly. Whichever way it was, I managed to uncover little about them from that time. Soon enough, though, they fell back into old ways. As I continued to scan police reports and news articles, their malfeasance again bubbled to the surface.

Each had rap sheets a mile long for various, yet predictable, ill deeds. There were burglary charges, assaults, and arrests for public intoxication and DUI. Polly had her share of prostitution stings, and it was clear she had gone back to the needle a time or two. Both had done time on various occasions, usually for a year at a stretch. I came upon a mugshot of Polly's. It was maybe fifteen years old, but she looked wildly different than she did on the day of our abrupt parting. Her face was thin and pock-marked by acne. Her hair had grown out and it lay limp along the sides of her face. That empty stare filled her eyes, but the ferocity was dialed back. She looked beaten, but not physically. What I mean to say is that she looked defeated. I'd be willing to bet that was the day when she finally realized that she had been a prey animal all along, and nothing more than a nuisance to the larger predators.

I stared into her hollow expression for quite a time, but eventually moved on with my search. I elected not to dig further into her past. I never really considered a fixed order on how I was going to see this undertaking done. Bill was convenient, a bit of poisonous serendipity, I suppose, but somehow, Polly was always going to be the last to go. Maybe something in my subconscious had told me that was the way it had to be. Maybe it was fate. Who knows? Sense and reason didn't have much say in these matters. I knew that much, anyway.

If the goal is to end a war, you kill the leader first and then consider whether or not to spare the soldiers. If the goal is to erase history, you kill everyone. In such a case, I know order don't much matter, really, but I wanted the architect to see it all dismantled before her own undoing. The war had burned itself out. It was on me to see to the history.

Criminal records, social media records, and internet data of most every variety in regards to Wayne seemed to have dried up a good piece back. Once I was confident that I had his correct last name, I went about rifling through obituary listings, but I couldn't even find him there. He just up and vanished.

The day wore on and I was getting discouraged. I knew I might not find them all, but the prospect of not being able to uncover the end of each tale needled me. I didn't much care if Wayne had died or if he was doing a twenty-to-life stretch. In either event, I would know where he was and I could take solace in his misery and misfortune. Not knowing, though, that I could not abide. This infernal trail I was blazing was essentially my life's work. I could not see it incomplete.

Luck is a funny thing. For a while, years, even, a turn of fortune can seem like a blessing, only to reveal its true implications decades later. It was such a mercurial contortion of fate that finally led me to Wayne. I came upon a newspaper article from the previous year that told of an unemployed man who had won the lottery and summarily donated his bounty to have a playground and park built for local children. I recognized the name but damn near blew off reading the file, figuring that this generous man could never be one and the same as the Wayne I once knew. Then again, he was always the kind one, the one with a conscience. He wasn't bad like the rest of us, he just found himself having to survive amongst the bad things.

As it went, old Wayne had been collecting disability for a number of years. I couldn't suss out a proper reason why, but judging from his picture in the paper, his weight was the source of his handicap. He looked enormous, not merely fat but bloated as well. He was living with a relative in a modest home in rural Michigan. By all accounts, his existence was quiet. The fluff piece about him told of how the local residents viewed him as a gentle giant. He didn't venture far from home, but every Sunday when the weather was nice, he and his aunt would visit the library and, after borrowing a few books, they would stop for ice cream on the way home.

I imagine very little was known about him before his donation. After such an event is when residents tend to change their opinions about the strangers who live among them. And so he, and others' perceptions of him, got dressed up for the article. That's just the way such things go. It's human nature. But it all spins back to luck, don't it? See, a poor man of meager means won the lottery. Then, he selflessly gives over said windfall to the community. In turn, he is instantly beloved and mythologized. So far, everybody's coming up aces. Now my good luck came in the form of that write-up. It was the map I needed to lead me to Wayne. And in that moment is when all that was once sweet fortune spoiled and turned sour. Wayne's good deed would become the catalyst of his undoing. So much for luck, huh?

Being as though Wayne seemed primed to suffer a massive heart attack at any moment, it would be logical to think that I would want to make haste toward Michigan. Instead, I found myself moving at a leisurely pace. Maybe I would get him. That would bring me satisfaction. But what if his internal organs beat me to the punch? It didn't bother me. However it was going to go down, I would know that he was put in the ground. If I missed him by a day or two, I could attend the funeral. I kinda fantasized about this possibility for a moment. At the least, I could visit his grave and see his life reduced to a small stone placed in a forgotten corner of a potter's field. I couldn't sweat the details. Whatever form fate took, I was paying a visit to The Great Lakes State.

I set a course north and drove off with the dawning of a new day. As the sun rose into a clear sky, it seemed to bring with it promises of calm hours. Taking the path less beaten, I exited the highway in favor of state routes. My pace would be slower, but the lush scenery around me and the feel of the breeze as it danced inside the car were pleasures too tempting to go without.

As I studied rolling swaths of farmland and quaint country towns, a sense of peace came for me. It wasn't a sensation I was accustomed to feeling. Even during my days with Riley, true serenity was hard to come by. Such a state of being is most likely a rare treat for the majority of us, but I got to thinking about why, on my way to perform a task that involved no peace, did I feel so contented?

I mulled this over a bit and came to the conclusion that I had, at last, accepted myself. I knew there weren't no good ending reserved for me. I didn't deserve as much and, so, all would be put square once everything was said and done. I looked forward to it, the closing of the circle, the shutting down of the cycle. Wayne was another cog in the machine that I intended to dismantle. Thinking about him in such a fashion gave me a purpose beyond the scope of my original goals. I felt a sense of obligation to all those I had wronged through the years. My direction might have been misguided, but this was my way of making amends. I then considered the end again, and all the ways it might come to deal with me. I found myself accepting of any scenario I could envision.

By afternoon, I was feeling a bit peckish. I swung into the parking lot of an old gas station. Just two pumps rose from the buckled asphalt and a small convenience store dotted the center of the property. The building was somewhat dilapidated, but in such a way as to look charming. Its best days were sunk into the past but, as it persisted into the age of tiny devices and high-speed internet, the store took on the role of time machine. It was a living relic, a reminder of life lived in times less sanitized.

I smiled at the sight of handmade signs advertising local produce that were tacked to the door. A set of hanging bells announced my arrival, and an old dog that rested behind the counter turned his head in my direction. Quickly becoming disinterested, the aging hound bedded back down. I received a warm hello from the clerk, a man who I imagined had run the station since the day of its opening. I milled around the narrow aisles and picked a bag of chips from a crooked shelf that also held batteries, motor oil, and other unrelated items. The lone upright cooler in the back had a door glazed over with fog but I found the appliance stocked with my soda of choice. I set my provisions on the counter and grabbed a free circular that told of local happenings. While the old man rung me out, I flipped through the flyer for the first and final time. I didn't really focus on any one thing. I was simply enjoying the freedom from concentration that this stop afforded me. But, hell, nothing lasts for long and the good things seem to have the shortest shelf life. That was my thinking once I heard a shaky and nervous voice come from the back of the store.

Not really hearing what was spoken, I turned. There, a good twenty paces behind me, was a girl. I couldn't put together a solid guess as to her age, but I figured her to be no younger than seventeen. She was a diminutive creature, the kind whose frame looked to have been constructed with glass tubes and other fragile materials in lieu of proper and sturdy bone. Her delicate body was similarly bereft of armor on the outside. Flip-flops formed the only barrier between the grime of the floor and her bare feet. A tight pair of jean shorts hung from her hip bones and the flannel top she wore was bound into a knot above her stomach. A black plastic hair band held back her locks and the accessory exaggerated the height of her forehead. I looked into her wild, unblinking eyes, and then to the gun in her hand.

"Give me—empty the drawer, and give me your money," she said nervously.

I turned to face her and eased back onto the counter. I heard as the old man began fumbling with the register, to which I raised my hand in a gesture intended to halt his action. He decoded my message and stilled himself. I had reservations about what next to do, even though I was wholly unafraid of the girl. My anxiety came solely from her spindly hand that clutched the gun. Her shaking was so intense that whatever aim she may have had would be nonexistent, but all that twitchin' could have easily led to an errant pull of the trigger. As I studied her further, I decided on taking my chances. Her arm was beginning to droop from the weight of the weapon as it were, and I was not of the mind to hand over a dime to a desperate teenager.

"What—what the fuck?" she muttered.

Of all the ways in which this scenario had played out in her mind, I'm guessing what actually went down wasn't anything like she had imagined. I was calling her bluff and, by all that lives and dies, she wasn't prepared to call mine.

"Give me your money," she said again, all sense of authority absent from her voice.

"Here, take it," I said. I pulled out my wallet, placed it beside me on the counter, and gave it a pat.

"Just throw it over, come on," she said, while waving the gun toward herself.

I smiled and said, "Oh, no, honey. You want it? You come and get it."

"I'll shoot," she said, tears appearing in her eyes.

"No, you won't, and you know it ain't gonna go your way if you scamper up here and try to take what's mine," I said.

"Mister, just give her what she wants," said the clerk.

"Hush now, old man. You were doing so good back there, just minding your business. I'd much appreciate it if you'd go back to doing just so. Me and the lady here are having a conversation," I said, never taking my eyes off the girl.

"Please, just…just give me the money," she whispered.

"Oh, you just broke rule number fucking one! Never ask for what you want with a gun in your hand. It's just bad form. Here I am, my life held in that sweaty little palm of yours, and you're the one doing the begging. Bad form, girl. Bad form," I said, to which her eyes filled with pleas and darted to the clerk.

"Don't look at him," I continued. "You were making to rob his store. He ain't helping you. And now you're wondering what happens next. You wanna know how it ends, don't you?" I asked, and she responded by sniffling and rubbing her nose with her arm.

"Alright, girl, listen up. If you want this money, you're going to have to earn it. So, option one is that you kill me, then you kill him, and maybe you have to kill a few more if some unlucky strangers just happen to wander in when things get hot. Now the tricky part about option one, here, is that you're easily identifiable. You find yourself in the starring role," I said, while motioning toward the security camera. "You're gonna get caught, sure as you're going to have to go and kill me for this money. That's guaranteed. And what's more? That's your best possible outcome for option one, presuming you don't get yourself killed in the process. So, what, a few hundred bucks, maybe a thousand today? Not too bad, I guess, but the only thing you're gonna buy with that money is the needle."

"I'm—I'm a minor," she said, mostly to herself, as she began to cry.

"Now, don't go thinking that matters. Five, fifteen, whatever you are, counts for nothing. The law don't have no sympathy for gutter-trash girls like you. You'll kill today and then die alone before your hair gets a chance to turn gray. Hey, I know that arm's getting tired. What say you lower your piece and give a listen to option two? Is that agreeable to you?" I asked and she nodded while lowering her gun.

"Thanks, honey, much appreciated," I said. "So, this here's how option two plays out. You're gonna set that gun down and walk your little ass out the door. You do that, and you keep walking, understand? There can't be no looking back. I'll be honest, option two ain't the sure thing that option one is. It's kind of a gamble. But, this could still turn out alright for you. Would you like to know how?"

She nodded again, laying the gun down atop an old ice cream freezer whose faulty compressor added an eerie ambiance to our exchange. She didn't speak but looked to me the way a lost child gazes at a crowd of strangers. She was a creature of the shallows, desperate for a way out of the depths into which she had waded.

"Nothing," I said.

"I—I don't understand. I just want to go home," she said, choking on her tears.

"Nothing is the payoff to this gamble. See, you can leave and, if you're lucky, nothing happens. Now, you don't have to worry about me. I'm going to forget all about you once you get on down the road. The question is, is he of the mind to turn you in?" I said, gesturing to the clerk. "I find myself in a generous mood, so tell you what. I'll see to it that this security tape goes away and I'll suggest to this fine gentleman here that he put today's events out of his mind. Is that amenable to you, old man?" I shouted, though he stood right behind me.

"Yes. Yes, sir," he replied with a start.

"You see, honey, all this may just work out yet. Go on, be on your way," I said as I pointed to the door.

She lowered her eyes and scampered for the exit. As she drew near to me nervousness almost sent her to the floor but, somehow, she remained on her feet. She gave the door a few frantic pulls before I leaned over and pushed it open. She gasped as I locked eyes with her again, our faces mere inches apart. With the door swung wide, she took to a sprint and quickly disappeared into the blazing light of the sun.

"Those cameras haven't worked in years," muttered the clerk after a loud exhale.

"Yeah, I figured as much," I said, while I strode over to the freezer and picked up the gun.

"Come on, now, ring me up. I got things to do," I said. I glanced up at the old man, whose color had drained away, leaving only a wrinkled face of white overrun by a network of thin veins. "Oh, sorry about that, I just didn't think the freezer the best place to leave this," I said as I laid the gun down in front of him.

"It's uh, it's on the house," he said wearily.

"Ain't nothing free. And don't go thinking I did what I did for you. See, if I don't pay, then I'll be in your debt, and I got no plans on coming back here. That is, unless you'd like to see me again?" I said, tapping my fingers on the butt of the gun.

"No. No, sir. That'll be $2.35," he replied in a whisper.

"Remember these dollars, old timer," I said as I slid three bucks across the counter. "You almost died for these and whatever paltry sum in floating around in that drawer. It hardly seems worth it when you really think about it, huh? Have yourself a fine day," I offered with a wink as I collected my change and exited the store.

Goddamn the influence of Paul Parker. That bastard's good intentions almost got me killed. Or, maybe, his steady hand had saved my life. What went down at the gas station may have been filtered through Kellen's attitude, but the calm that underscored the events came courtesy of Paul. Perhaps the two sides of myself came together perfectly to see me out of a jam that would have otherwise ended in blood. I can't say for sure, but there is one thing I know: Paul's good intentions sowed the seeds of a bitter harvest to come. I survived and, as such, I was alive to continue the hunt and extermination of Wayne and Polly.

By late afternoon I was south of Battle Creek, Michigan and near my target. I elected not to immediately pay a visit to Wayne. Instead, I found myself a cheap motel. It looked to be the type of place that serves as a crash site for the exhausted and as a stage for the illicit goings-on of transients. Such environs never put me off, but I was pleased to discover that the exterior of the motel belied its true quality. My room was clean and the staff were friendly and helpful. Hell, even the water pressure of the shower was good.

Recognizing that I was no longer an infernal young man, I admitted to myself that I was in need of a breather. In short order, I had killed a man, recused a child, and was nearly executed. Such things will wear on the mind, especially when there's nothing but heavy lifting still to come. I used some idle time to gather my thoughts and brush up on the details of Wayne's whereabouts. Fixing my mind to his murder proved a difficult task to master. It troubled me that I again became conflicted about moving forward with my plans. This was an unforeseen obstacle, but one I resolved to overcome all the same.

I waited until night came down before I took back to the road. My course sent me through a charming suburb replete with even sidewalks and manicured lawns. As I drove on, I passed by a strip mall and a string of trendy chain restaurants. By the time I had reached the outer rings of town, the sheen began to fall away. What I next came to find wasn't decay, though. It was simply old. The community in which I found myself surely existed long before the countryside was cleared for developments and anchor stores. As I cruised by mom-and-pop shops and farm stands closed for the evening, I took to thinking about Riley and our life left behind in Stone Horse. Regrettably, I had no time to pine for things gone away. That was a luxury I could no longer afford.

Atop a long road that wove into the hills, and with wind turbines slowly turning in the distance of the dark sky, I exited my vehicle. The street on which Wayne and his aunt's home sat snaked off from the main road and wound down into a valley. I walked along the guardrail and studied the dead-end street and the small collection of houses that dotted it. Each had been built far enough from the other to insure the privacy of their occupants. Deeds banal and those of a less savory nature could be committed without the complications brought about by nosy neighbors.

Ominous as it seemed, Wayne's place of residence was the last house on the left. Butted against the edge of his yard was a rusted fence of chainlink. It cordoned off a dirt road that seemingly lead to nothing but the scraped plans of failed enterprise. This picture of a future abandoned proved fitting. Here, at the end of the line, is where I would find Wayne.

There were tire impressions in the gravel of the driveway, but no car was present. Amber light bled out from a ground floor window of the small, single-family dwelling. The grass under my step was patchy, but in need of mowing. Old paint curled and flaked from the porch columns and the aluminum siding bore dents and a smattering of algae that told of its age. I stood before the front door with my finger on the buzzer but hesitated to ring the bell. From what I had gathered, Wayne seemed wholly dependent on the goodwill of his aunt to see him to places hither and yon. With no car in sight, I imagined her to be out, but I hadn't bothered to try and confirm when she might be out of the house.

Admittedly, I had slacked on my homework. I had already resolved that if she was home, I would do her no harm. She had no role in this play, but her presence would complicate matters. If I followed through with my intentions, she could potentially see me delivered into the hands of the law and all but guarantee the end of my quest. To send Bill and Wayne to the worms but leave Polly free from reprisal was unacceptable. To dwell on thoughts of consequences would only serve to stall me. I would navigate the dark paths of the unknown if and when they appeared under my feet. Hoping desperately that Wayne was home alone, I rang the bell.

A deep bellow instructed me to see myself in, and this voice I recognized as Wayne's. I eased the door open, and, brushed in soft light, I walked slowly over the carpet. The state of the inside of the home was not at all what I had expected. It was tidy, pleasantly scented, and meticulously ordered. Every picture was hung and displayed with obvious purpose and all the assorted knick-knacks were free of dust. Furthermore, when I turned into the living room, it was far from the glutton's den I had imagined. There weren't empty bags of potato chips strewn about the floor. Stains and tears were absent from the furniture. The TV wasn't tuned to a daft reality program. In fact, it wasn't on at all.

"Kellen, is that you?" Wayne asked as he peered at me over his glasses and through the dark. His query was framed as a proper question, but I felt that he was fairly confident as to its answer. Seated in a large recliner, he was dressed in a plain t-shirt and sweatpants. Still, somehow, his choice of attire didn't make him appear like a common slob. He wore these items because a man of his size has few options when it comes to clothing. Though primarily housebound, Wayne seemed to keep himself in order. His hair was combed neatly and his beard was trimmed short and even.

"Yeah, Wayne, it's me," I said as I seated myself on a couch opposite him. For a time, I said nothing and he did the same. Instead, I studied his environment, his world, as it were. In a way, it seemed he was allowing me the time to do so. A shelf to his back had its capacity rating strained by scientific magazines, books on philosophy, poetry, and biographies of people largely forgotten, but responsible for shaping the world nonetheless. An end table to his right supported a collection of puzzle books whose challenges were far removed from the relative ease of such dime-store amusements. We may have remained silent, but an old yet elegant record player was alive with the sounds of Tchaikovsky.

"Kellen, I think I know. No, I know why you're here," he said finally.

"Do you now, Wayne?" I asked.

"I never liked what we did to you. I just wanted the home invasions to stop," he said quietly.

"Yeah, well, maybe you should have tossed Polly over with me."

"I don't want to talk about her, Kellen. That'll just make me think of what I was like when we were young. I get sad when I think about things like that," said Wayne.

"Is that what all this is, then?" I asked, gesturing to the books. "Have you collected all this stuff just so you have to think so damn hard about other things that there's no time left to think about who you used to be?"

"I just like them, and, besides, I don't get out much," he said with a chuckle.

I grew quiet again. I hadn't prepared for finding myself at a loss for words or actions when coming upon Wayne. I had pictured him obnoxious and repugnant. A beast ready-made for slaughter. Instead, I found a thinking man, and a man handicapped but at peace with his limitations. By my estimation, he had used his mind to overcome his troubles and in turn had made himself into a figure worthy of pity and envy in equal measure.

"Kellen, my aunt will probably be home in a couple of hours," he said with some urgency in his tone.

"What makes you think that worries me?"

"Because you're here to kill me. Why else would you be here?" he stated flatly.

"I suppose if you've sussed that out, I should at least have courtesy enough not to bullshit you. If I'm being honest, though, I don't know how I feel about all this," I said, my mind utterly conflicted.

"I can't help you feel better about killing, just like all these books can't help me feel no better about the things I done. We just have to live with our pasts. That's the worst part for me," he said.

"Do you want to die, Wayne?" I asked, truly curious as to his answer.

"I have wanted to die from time to time. It's the sort of feeling that changes with the day, you know? Maybe I would have done it myself. I was always too scared, though. The violence, Kellen, I just can't deal with the violence."

As Wayne said this, I saw as he teared up. He was sincerely

haunted by who he once was. That impressionable child bullied into acts of atrocity by the animals that circled him. If we hadn't known each other previously, I would have connected with him all the same in that moment. I knew what it was to be shackled to the deeds of years gone by. I knew the agony of being bound to fate. I knew the desperation of having no escape route on which to run. I knew the specter of punishment, the way it gnaws at the soul as it waits patiently for the day when the cost of former ills is to be collected.

"Can mercy and murder be one and the same?" I asked as I glanced to his books.

"Ambrose Bierce once said that there are four kinds of homicide: felonious, excusable, justifiable, and praiseworthy. So, I guess you can decide which one mine might be, although Ambrose didn't say nothing about mercy. I don't know, Kellen, maybe there just ain't no mercy set aside for people like us," said Wayne.

"Maybe not," I said, quietly and in a tone that exposed the sorrow that stirred within me. We sat quietly for another moment, just looking to one another. We had the type of conversation that can only be had between people who have shared in horrible experiences. Nothing needed to be spoken, but a dialogue was going on all the same. After it seemed we had come to common ground, I gave Wayne a smile. There was no malice in my expression. It was more of a shrug of the face, a way to say goodbye. Not to a friend, but to someone less-than who also happened to be so much more. He returned my gesture with a nod, to which I rose from the couch and made for the kitchen.

I stuck Wayne in the chest a couple of times with a common carving knife. I doubt my aim was sound enough to find his heart but, all the same, he died quickly and with nary a sound. It is at this point that I would like to speak of him no more. I can't find no earthly reason to go on about this subject further, but there was something about the actual killing that has unsettled me.

Backing up a bit, to the time before I had decided on my weapon of choice, I stood in his aunt's kitchen gripped by indecision. I fiddled about and wasted time. I swept my eyes over a set of porcelain dogs that served as salt and pepper shakers. They were bookended by cookbooks and a stack of bills that I figured to be overdue, given the large quantity. There were pictures on the fridge of Wayne, a homely woman I assumed to be his aunt, and assorted children. A few dishes swam in discolored water and, above the sink, there was a framed picture of a quote. Beneath the glass and a coating of dust it read, *No God, no peace. Know God, know peace.* For reasons I can't explain, that sentiment gave me a shiver. The simplistic foolishness of such a notion grated at me, angered me. Ain't nothing so easy. I knew that much and so did Wayne.

I entertained ways of murdering him that had a chance of going unnoticed. I thought that if I suffocated him by means of a trash bag or pillow that perhaps when he was found it would be assumed that the big guy's heart had up and given out. But then I worked my thinking around to how I might give him a more memorable send-off. If foul play was clearly his cause of death, Wayne would be, for a little while, anyway, mythologized further. His untimely death, paired with the charity that he had shown to his community, would just about guarantee him a permanent place in the town's history. An outpouring of love would precede his burial. Maybe the residents that had benefitted from his generosity would band together to petition the mayor to rename a street or a park in Wayne's honor. I'm not sure if he deserved all that, but I had to consider the possibility that he might. I also had to ponder on whether or not he deserved to be murdered at all, but, with a knife in my hand, I suppose I had already settled on an answer.

What happened next was utterly unexpected and it caught me unawares, but my decision was made, my purpose set. When I emerged from the kitchen, Wayne went into hysterics. He set eyes on that knife and his resolve fell apart. In the time it took me to walk across the room and stick him, he begged, blubbered, and cried. He made moves to defend himself, but my strike was too quick to allow for much resistance. He knew what was coming. He had resigned himself to it and, still, he sank into panic once it came time for the reckoning. I was shaken by this but, Wayne had said so himself, he just couldn't deal with the violence.

21. All The King's Horses And All The King's Men

I lit out of Michigan and pushed back east. In the days before I sent Wayne to his end, I had brushed up on Polly. Digging up what could be found online, I sifted through the wreckage of her past. From what I could gather, she had traveled south some years after my swan dive off the overpass. I knew not her reasons for abandoning Ohio, if there were any at all, but I suspected she was running. Probably from the law, surely from a host of undesirables that wished her harm, but, mostly, I suspected she was running from herself.

Her flight from the north saw her land among the tangle of red clay roads of rural Mississippi. For a time, she lived with a woman, some twenty years Polly's senior, who the local newspaper referred to as her lover. People became many things to Polly, but using a word like love to describe anything that got pulled into her orbit just seemed rather vulgar. Whatever the particulars of their relationship might have been I can't say, but they were certainly a match. The girlfriend had been busted for drugs and aggravated assault, and she also had a sex trafficking charge. I was curious as to the finer points of that violation, but they must have gotten sucked away in the undertow of the endless news cycle.

It was unclear how long they shacked with one another, but the end was spelled out for me in black and white. As it turned out, the two of them tried their hands at cooking up meth inside the rusted-out single-wide that they shared. On a humid night in August, the cops kicked in the doors and hauled them both away. Gina, that was the other chick's name, she got ten years due to priors, and Polly was sentenced to half that time. I knew Polly had plenty of priors herself. How she got away with nothing more than a glorified slap on the wrist is a puzzle that will always confound me.

A few pictures of the bust were linked from the article and, as I looked at the images, my feelings were of equal parts disgust and satisfaction. The latter reaction sprung from an obvious source; I was happy to see Polly suffer. However, my disgust came from a part of my mind murkier to define. The blighted condition of the trailer, the haggard look of Polly and her companion, the disheveled nature of their clothes all spoke to a sense of desperation. The scheme to manufacture and distribute drugs wasn't one of Polly's brilliant ideas. This was an impetuous grasp in the dark, a rash bid for survival, nothing more. It was then that I came to peel away the mystification I had erroneously surrounded Polly with in my memories. She was a bottom-feeder dying at the bottom of the world.

Later news articles told me of her parole three years into her sentence. What followed were transgressions of a predictable nature. The busts for things once beneath her came rattling along: petty theft, drunken disorderly, vagrancy. That last one really stuck into me. it must have demolished any sense of self that Polly had left. She had come to a point in her life where simply the state of her existence was deemed unacceptable by the world around her. Polly Parker, they said, you belong nowhere.

Such events break people. They reduce formerly complete beings down to scraps and brittle fragments. For a lot of folks, this is the end announcing its presence into their lives, even if actual finality has yet to arrive. There ain't nothing quite so efficient at burying people as the absence of hope, it seems.

It was about this time in my research that I began to doubt if I would ever find Polly under all the rubble. As far as internet archives were concerned, she had vanished. I entertained the idea that she had died, forgotten and anonymous in some basement or back alley. Maybe all the drugs and assorted damage that she had done to herself saw her withering away in a derelict state-run asylum. Perhaps she plunged further south, down to some impoverished village in Latin America where she could fade away, like a noxious gas into the wide, empty sky. I had about resigned myself to the fact that my quest would go unfinished. I was convinced that the time for me to set this on the square had run out. I knew I was chasing a phantom, and then I checked Facebook.

Polly Parker-Marconi. I almost skipped right over this entry but, as I came across very few *Polly Parkers*, I decided to give it a click and see what was what. I suspect that it was boredom, more than anything else, that led me to look into this mother of two. There seemed no other sound reason to investigate. Nothing about this woman's profile suggested that she was in fact the creature I sought. I figured finding Polly on social media was a shot in the black as it was. I had considered that traces of her could be unearthed from rummaging through old listings on escort sites, but never would I have imagined actually tracking her down on something as common and domestic as Facebook. But there she was.

Her profile picture was an image that looked ripped from a cheap brochure, dripping with promises of family fun to be had at a beach resort or amusement park. Her hair, still blonde but seemingly lightened, was fixed into a style often favored by respectable white women who make their homes in the suburbs. Her lips were parted in a wide smile and every visible tooth was white and straight. A pair of sunglasses was perched above her forehead, the sinking sun glistening in the distance. To each side of her was a child, both girls, both with syrupy grins and sun-yellow hair. They clung to Polly with genuine affection, and it seemed she had taken the liberty of adding a little flair to this sweet snapshot. In large bubble letters, the word *love* was applied over the bottom of the picture.

In a dimly lit and sparsely populated public library, I leaned back in my chair. This was no easy act of reclining. It was more akin to being forced back by the power of a blast wave. Everything about what I found felt wrong, like a grievous and cosmic error. How had it come to be that this monstrosity of blood and flesh, this beast, had settled into an ordinary and pleasurable existence? Yeah, it was little more than dumb luck and a damaged brain that gifted me a life with Riley, but Polly didn't have the luxury of such an excuse. She knew full well who she was. She even kept her maiden name. Somewhere along the line, she had stopped running and faced down her reflection. Among her social media posts of kiddie pictures and recipes, there were entries, eloquently written and heartfelt, that spoke of addiction and mental illness.

Perhaps what was most startling to me was that I could barely locate the death and vacancy that once occupied her stare. It was barely there. Maybe only eyes such as mine could detect it. She was indeed remade, taken apart down to the basics of her construction and put back together in the proper fashion. I had no doubt this transformation was done by her own hand. I guess if she had retained one thing from the old days, it was that iron nerve.

For me, the hits just kept coming. She had gotten married a handful of years back to a man who worked in finance, whatever that means. He appeared a ready-made family man. Successful, but grounded. Judging by his own profile, he seemed to be well-liked and honestly kind. A handsome face with the modern American dad-bod. He had a daughter from a previous marriage. The other kid was all theirs. I skimmed across pictures of the happy couple vacationing on a beach and slamming cake into each other's faces at their wedding. Polly wore white.

I got the impression that he knew of her past, not the finer details, but he knew enough about Polly that she would be able to lay her head down at night and go into sleep not feeling guilty over keeping secrets from her husband. And what was more? Their union seemed a true marriage. This wasn't some May-December arrangement where an old man pays the way for a pretty girl, decades his junior. This man, for reasons indefinable, loved Polly Parker for all that she was. And, though she had cleaned up, the dope does its damage. Her skin may have been clear, her teeth got fixed somewhere along the way, but even under the makeup, the drugs had carved their tells across her face. Polly was attractive, but I might hesitate to call her pretty. She was flawed, complicated, and knew what it meant to be fucked up. And, yet, she was loved for, and in spite of, all of it.

However impossible it was to believe the information I had already found, what I was soon to learn would test every fiber of credulity. My former junk puppet had got herself an education and found work in graphic design. If the bio on her employer's website was to be believed, she was rather successful in her field. Marriage, a family, an education, and a career. These were all fulfilling aspects of life that I never imagined Polly would have. Furthermore, to the Polly I once knew, these were just *things*, vulgar and of little desire. My astonishment was matched only by how tirelessly productive she seemed to be, as I came to find that she also volunteered at an animal shelter and was an active PTA member at her daughters' school.

The day around me melted away and time became a thing of no consequence. As I saw Polly reassembled, I found myself being taken apart. What she had achieved made my own turn of character seem trite by comparison. Due to injury, I managed to behave myself for a while. She turned everything inside out and made clean all that was once filthy. It was about this time that I was again forced to contemplate my stated objective. Could I kill this woman and orphan her children? Did she, after all this time, still deserve punishment for the sins of the past? I struggled mightily with these questions but, ultimately, the whims of Paul would lose out to the law of reciprocity.

To move forward wasn't something I came to decide quickly or with ease. My mind was also not favored by feelings of calm once the decision had been made. In many respects, I was torn apart. However, what tipped the scales of condemnation against Polly was Polly herself. She was the architect of this implausible transformation while still shackled to all that she once had been. With all the ghosts chained to her back, it was a wonder she could even rise from her bed each morning. Once I had wormed my way around to such thoughts, she became more monstrous than before. I came to view her as a corrupt and failed creator, a villain under masks of modernity, a maker of wretches who would soon know justice at the hands of one of her own beasts.

22. Killing Death

A few days later I was sitting in the parking lot of a shopping mall located in a busy suburb of Pittsburgh. I had learned of the house that Polly called home, familiarized myself with her work schedule, and tailed a few car lengths behind her as she left the house that morning. Before this pursuit, I watched as the kids walked to the mouth of their cul-de-sac street to catch the school bus. I winced as Polly gave her husband a kiss as he set off to work, and I smiled as she never once looked over her shoulder.

I parked the Lumina a few rows over from Polly and watched as she checked her makeup in the rearview mirror. She drove a late model SUV with the names of her children displayed on the rear windshield under generic images of ballet dancers. The rear bumper was decorated by an OBX sticker and a graphic that read *salt life*. There was even a 26.2 decal, advertising to the world that someone in the family had finished a marathon. Running. This felt a fitting activity for Polly to take up.

She stepped out, wearing a pair of white capri pants and a blouse that was equal parts professional and sexy. Confidently, she strode her way across the lot. She had on a pair of pumps that had heels fashioned from cork. Her legs swung like scissor blades as she walked. She slung her purse over her shoulder and lit a cigarette. It was a relief to see that some flaw or vice had stuck with her. My eyes followed her as she made for the entrance. Just before the clean, beige doors of the mall, she snuffed the butt out on the bottom of her shoe, tossed it in the trash, and disappeared into Macy's.

I made my way back to Polly's street. I was full of jittery indecision, but I dared not tarry in the car. Although I had been smart enough to park a considerable distance from Polly's house over the course of the past week, I imagined the presence of an unknown vehicle had gathered some suspicion. I left it a couple of streets over and walked as casually as my legs would allow. As I wound my way towards Polly's house, there was an old lady tending to a garden next door. A part of me became as a machine as I strolled over and happily introduced myself as Polly's cousin. I felt outside myself as I made light conversation and complimented the old woman on the condition of her lawn. A hot, gurgling broth of self-loathing welled inside me over how natural it felt to utterly disguise myself as something other than a monstrous creature but, still, my gums kept bumping. Soon enough she bid me a good day and I left her behind to the needs of flowers.

As I turned my back, the world seemed to change and disintegrate around me. It was like the sky turned black and every pool in every birdbath and pond grew yellow and acidic. The smooth concrete driveway under my step seemed to buckle, crack, and dissolve, the graves of those forgotten rising up through the fissures. I swore I watched as the trees shook loose their leaves and flung their roots up from the soil, as if to escape the bitter taste of bad earth. I felt alone, then, walking down the darkest road of fate toward the end of days.

Maybe I had been taken by a bit of Bill's fire and brimstone fervor. I suppose this weird episode could have been influenced by the story of The Four Horsemen. Our old gang once fancied ourselves as such beings, but we were vermin, failed imposters, and phonies. Still, though, we were linked together all the same, and even myths meet their end. Why should the four of us fare any better? As War, I had done my part, lived up to my nature. I had slain my comrades. It was time for the reckoning, to kill Death or be killed by it. I thought of the possibility of failure and of Polly continuing to worm her way through the world unchecked. I believe I have said it before, this I could not abide. It was my charge to set this right, to kill Polly. As for after what demanded doin' got done, well, what's left for War?

By the time I had reached the backyard, things more or less worked their way back to normal. I shook off the last of my daydreams and observed my surroundings. A swing set glistened in the sun and an iron glider bench sat beneath a row of pine trees that lined the back of the property. A narrow flowerbed ran along the edge of the driveway and among the colorful bulbs, a large stone had been placed. It was engraved with the words, *The Marconis.* As I climbed the steps of the back porch, a light breeze danced through the trees and stirred a song from a set of wind chimes. The door was locked but, having swiped their hide-a-key a couple of days back, I saw myself inside the house.

The door opened up into the kitchen. A bowl of fresh fruit and a vase of flowers spotted an island that was finished with a polished stone countertop and flanked by a pair of stools. The appliances were sleek and modern, with the fridge decorated by photos of the kids and pictures they had drawn. Above the sink, which held not one dirty dish, there was a plaque. Down the center of this wooden ornament were the words *live, laugh, love.*

Figuring I still had some time to kill before Polly returned, I strolled about the house. I was certain that in some dark corner I would come to find traces of the girl I once knew. Unlikely as it then seemed, I almost expected to find bodies in the basement or, at the least, a dope stash in a dresser drawer. But there was nothing. The walls were white, the carpets were clean, the bathroom vanity supported a bowl of potpourri, and every bed was made. I could not find a crack in this perfect middle-class veneer, because this wasn't simply a coating thrown up over decay. What I had witnessed was genuine.

I began to feel tired as I reflected on all that I had forsaken in the undertaking of this meaningless quest. It was like I was a bottle with a crack at the bottom. All that was within me seemed to leak out, leaving only emptiness. I eased myself into an armchair in the living room and felt my heart turn brittle and break. I had to admit that Polly had changed and I hadn't, not really. I tried to remind myself that she needed to answer for all that she had done, not just to me, but to others as well. It was of no use. If there existed such a way for her to atone for the transgressions of her past, what more could she have done? I thought to leave, to exit the house as quietly as I had entered, my trespass never to be known. I had this fantasy of wandering off into the wilderness to disappear, not in any realistic sense, this was more of a desire to simply be absorbed into nature. I wanted desperately an exit from the world of man. Tears broke from my eyes as I went to rise when, at once, I heard the rattling of keys. I peered into the kitchen and witnessed the door knob as it turned. From my pocket, I pulled my gun.

"Hi, Polly," I said to her as she walked in, her arms full of shopping bags.

Everything in her grasp was loosed and tumbled about across the floor. Juice from a shattered jar, and the slime from a dozen broken eggs, sloshed together and ruined each item they touched. Polly stood before the mess, wide-eyed and rigid as a statue. As I looked into her eyes for the first time in twenty years, I was made witness to something I never thought would have existed within her: fear. This was perhaps the most profound change that she had undergone. Momentarily, I shared her stillness, but, with just the twitching of her limbs, I again found my purpose.

"Sit down," I said sternly, as she half-turned in an effort to flee. "Sit down, Polly, or I will fill you with bullets."

She lowered herself onto one of the stools, a nervously whispered "*okay*" leaving her lips. I took the seat opposite her and the two of us stayed quiet as we studied one another. Like me, I imagine she was asking herself a myriad of questions and summarily crafting answers, both logical and otherwise. We looked at each other, but not in the way that people who once intimately knew one another and had ultimately become estranged typically do. I don't think we even gazed upon each other as people. Our stares were more akin to separate forms of alien life observing creatures near impossible to define.

"Kellen, please," she began quietly.

"Begging?" I asked, "That's not like the Polly I know."

"I'm not that girl anymore. I left her behind a long time ago," she said earnestly.

"That don't change nothing. You gotta answer for the things you've done," I said, tapping the butt of the gun on the countertop.

"Please, don't do this. I have children," she said, pressing her palm onto her chest as tears filled her eyes.

"So? You killed a child," I said. Polly twitched as though, for just a second, she had been electrocuted. The color left her face and I watched as sweat broke from her pores. Seemingly without warning, she vomited on the floor. With haste, she snapped herself back upright and looked at me as she swam among a mix of dread and agony.

"How, how…?" she asked, mostly to herself, with her palms opened to the air above and her face twisted by pain.

"Wayne told me, all them years ago."

"Fuck him," she said angrily.

"So, it's actually true," I said. "You know, for all this time, I kinda doubted that story. I always thought that there weren't nothing you considered off-limits, no matter how horrible. But, for some reason, I always questioned whether or not you went and killed that girl. Now I know, but it don't really change much, does it?"

"There are days," she started, with a shaky exhale. "Days upon days, that I can barely look at my girls without crying. I can usually hold it together in front of them, but it all gets to be too much sometimes. I think about that little girl, and her mother, and everything she never got to do because of me. It…it never leaves me."

"If she were the only one you hurt, maybe you could be forgiven. But feeling guilty over one crime don't make you any less of a monster, Polly."

"Fuck you." She said this sharp and slow. Polly then clenched her jaw with such ferocity that I could hear the sound of her teeth as they ground together. Her eyes were red rimmed and wet with tears, but I saw that look of death, old and stale, as it filled her stare.

"I don't take this lightly," I said. "People like you and me, the things that we are, we're like savages that wound up living in modern times. There's just no place for us. And we don't change, not really. Shit, even if we could, we can't undo all the wrong we done. Did you really think that you'd never have to answer for all the pain you caused?"

"I wasn't the only one that tossed you off that fucking bridge," she said with a snarl.

"They're already in the ground." Polly shuddered as I relayed the news. Maybe, to her, what was happening wasn't quite real. It may have been a defense mechanism, but I think she opted not to confront the obvious reason for my visit. But with what I had said, there was no more denying my purpose in her home.

"Fine, I'm a piece of shit, so what? So are you," she snapped.

"I'll be dealt with. I know that. It has to be done to set right all the wrongs we committed. I don't like it any more than you do. It's just the way things have to be. I'm sorry, Polly, and not just about this. I'm sorry for a lot of things. But I gotta be honest, I'm tired of talking," I said, and, as I did, I felt as my own eyes grew misty.

"Please, Kellen, please don't do this. Break my legs, cut up my face, I don't care, just don't take me away from my children," she pleaded.

"You've done this to yourself," I said, coldly.

"You're worse than me. You do this, you're worse than me," she said as she hardened her tone and pointed a finger at me. Her nails were smooth and painted blue. In that moment, I expected them to grow into talons.

"If you think of yourself as some righteous vigilante, you're wrong," Polly continued. "You're scum, a pathetic loser who can't leave the past behind. It's done. Fuck it. And don't act like everyone we knocked over was innocent. Most of them had it coming, anyway. Get over it, get over me, get over yourself. Stick that gun in your fucking mouth and blow your brains out all over my kitchen. I'll gladly clean up the mess with a smile on my face. You know, I'm glad you lived. I'm glad you never found happiness. You deserve to be the miserable, hateful, useless pile of shit that you are."

I looked to her and knew the time to put an end to our dance had come. She was running out of lies. All that was left was venom and truth. To survive, she would happily assume her former nature, her true nature. I saw her face as it tensed, the way an animal's does when it bares its teeth. I watched as a vein in her forehead thickened and came to the surface of her skin. Though the movements of her eyes were nearly indiscernible, I noticed as they strayed from my gun and to anything that she could employ as a weapon. I had found what I came to find. Polly Parker. To get what she wanted, she would do anything. Be it the murder of a child to alleviate boredom, or my execution to ensure that she'd make her daughter's next soccer game, it didn't matter. Polly came first.

"Tell me something," she said to me, sounding alarmingly calm. "Where have you been all this time?"

"I suppose that's a fair question. I could honor it as a last wish sorta thing, but you don't get to ask that, Polly. The fact is, it don't matter anymore. I will tell you something, though. I've changed, too, just enough to put the things that need hurting and the things that don't into separate piles. I will promise you this. I won't let the kids find you," I said.

With those words, I watched as Polly crumbled. She wept

quietly but was clearly strangled by a great sorrow all the same. She let me see the vulnerability, pain, and regret that had been as familiar to her as her own shadow. The game was done, and she knew it. She'd caused enough damage in her time to know what it meant to stare into the point of no return. She never did look at me again, but she didn't close her eyes either. Instead, she fixed her stare to something over my shoulder. In this time, our shared and final hour of desolation, I took one last look at Polly. The tears that ran through her makeup, the trembling of her lips, the unsteady breath that pumped into and out of her lungs. All of this was genuine. All of it tragic, pitiable, and cruel. In that moment, if there was one being on earth able to buy my compassion and sympathy, it was Polly.

I shot her in the face.

23. Clear

True to my word, I saw to it that Polly's children would be spared the irreparable horror of finding their mother's body. Before I took my leave of the house, I alerted the authorities to the murder and the location of where the deed got done. The door had nearly closed behind me when I remembered the stare Polly had fixed in her last moments. I peered back into the kitchen and to the fridge that was at my back when the reckoning came. There, among a calendar and assorted coupons, was a card. It was nothing more than cardboard and crayon. Scrawled across the front in the penmanship of a child was the sentiment that Polly had given the entirety of her focus. It read, simply, *mommy, please don't be sad.*

I left the house, but I did so without haste. I would be caught soon enough. There was no need to hurry. Besides, getting away with what I had done was never in the plan. I still had a responsibility to tend to. I had to get mine. For that, I had time enough.

I wound my way closer to the city before leaving the Lumina along the sidewalk of a narrow side street. I emerged from the shadows of the alley and into the sunlight. The day was warm, but not unpleasant. The air swirled with the warring scents of roasted coffee, warm butter and syrup from the griddles of a nearby diner, and bus exhaust. I walked among regular citizens who went about the day's errands and work, ignorant of the creature in their midst. I smiled as I passed a young woman. She was carrying a small but robust dog. He seemed aged and must have tired early of the walk. With a group of school children, I made my way across the street and turned onto the pedestrian pathway of a bridge.

It appeared before me like the essence of justice formed from concrete and steel. As this goliath spanned the river under my step, its arches looked to be a massive set of scales. They were painted gold, a reminder to me that a payment was due to set right the balance. I walked to the center and gazed out over the water, over the trees, and to the sky. I began to reflect on my life and what a waste it had been. As strange as it might sound, I felt a kinship with Lazarus. He was plucked from death and raised back up to live again, much as I was reunited with my true self once my memories had returned. I didn't need them back. Once was enough. Maybe Lazarus felt the same way. Perhaps he was ready for the ground and rued bitterly his resurrection. It was as though I had once been plucked from the grave as well, only to feel the nagging desire to crawl back in. Truth be told, it was always where I belonged.

Cars and cyclists whizzed on by and the breeze blew all about me. Far below, it caused the leaves in the trees to dance and shake. The clouds shifted and came apart overhead. Birds and butterflies skittered through the air while the river below continued its incessant roll. About the only thing that seemed static was the city. It loomed before me, an iron judge fixing an accusatory glare onto the condemned.

The buildings, with their innumerable windows and doors, spoke to me of endless possibilities, all of which were now shut to me. Perhaps, all along, the paths open to me were many. Such a prospect no longer mattered. I had walked a wrong road, and all that could have been was laid out before me but held at lengths unreachable. More than possibility, the image of the city spoke to me of the end.

I may be leaving, but I'm leaving something behind. This manifesto, this document, this chain of sins. Whatever it may be, I leave it here, not to garner pity, not to plead for understanding. I leave this behind in an effort to be exposed. Riley, the kids, Polly's family, all of them, are owed the truth. Everything I have done is crooked. There ain't no straightening it out now. The ability to do right has eluded me absolutely, so the least I can do is be honest. The funny thing is, I'm not sure if I even got that right. Maybe I've just been telling stories, but what does it all come down to? Most times the truth wounds deeper than the lies.

As I look into the water below, I find myself thinking, but not about regret or shame. I'm not even thinking about the possibility of damnation. I have just one thought, a hope, wedged into the center of my mind. When I sink under the waves, may that great river be endless and flow over me, to scrub me away, until the water runs clear.

—END—

Acknowledgements

Thanks to Meghan Miller for her excellent editing work and for being a joy to work with.

Special thanks to Christine Anderson, Brian Barna, Sue Murphy, Elizabeth Rome, Ralph Salla, Michele Vos, and Christopher Wood for their early support of Curse.

Extra special thanks to my friends and family, especially my parents, my sister, and my amazing girlfriend, Rachel. You guys are awesome.

About the Author

Rich Hayden was born and raised in Pittsburgh, PA. He still lives in the area with Rachel and two cats, affectionately nicknamed Nippy and Chicken.

Other titles by Rich Hayden

CrimeSpree – 2015

ISBN# 978-0-9963969-1-2 (paperback)

ISBN# 978-0-9963969-0-5 (E-book)

Curse – 2016

ISBN# 978-0-9963969-3-6 (paperback)

ISBN# 978-0-9963969-2-9 (E-book)

Website

http://hayden428.wixsite.com/richhayden

www.ingramcontent.com/pod-product-compliance
Lightning Source LLC
Chambersburg PA
CBHW050741230626
47052CB00004BA/965